Treasure Island

Treasure Island

ROBERT LOUIS STEVENSON

Condensed and adapted by
Nancy Fletcher-Blume

Illustrated by
Jerry Dillingham

Cover illustrated by
Ezra Tucker

Plate colorization by
Jerry Dillingham

Dalmatian Press

The Dalmatian Press Great Classics for Children
have been adapted and illustrated with care and thought,
to introduce you to a world of famous authors, characters, ideas,
and stories that have been loved for generations.

Editor — Kathryn Knight
Creative Director — Gina Rhodes
And the entire classics project team of Dalmatian Press

TREASURE ISLAND
Copyright © 2004 Dalmatian Press, LLC

The DALMATIAN PRESS name and logo are trademarks
of Dalmatian Press, LLC, Franklin, Tennessee 37067
No part of this book may be reproduced or copied in any form
without the written permission of Dalmatian Press.

ISBN: 1-40371-252-2 (M) 1-40371-387-1 (X)
13567

05 06 07 08 09 LBM 15 14 13 12 11 10 9 8 7 6 5 4 3

A note to the reader—

A classic story rests in your hands. The characters are famous. The tale is timeless.

This Great Classic for Children by Dalmatian Press has been carefully condensed and adapted from the original version (which you really *must* read when you're ready for every detail). We kept the well-known phrases for you. We kept the author's style. And we kept the important imagery and heart of the tale.

Literature is terrific fun! It encourages you to think. It helps you dream. It is full of heroes and villains, suspense and humor, adventure and wonder, and new ideas. It introduces you to writers who reach out across time to say: "Do you want to hear a story I wrote?"

Curl up and enjoy.

DALMATIAN PRESS
GREAT CLASSICS FOR CHILDREN

ALICE'S ADVENTURES IN WONDERLAND

ANNE OF GREEN GABLES

BLACK BEAUTY

THE CALL OF THE WILD

THE STORY OF
DOCTOR DOLITTLE

HEIDI

THE ADVENTURES OF
HUCKLEBERRY FINN

A LITTLE PRINCESS

LITTLE WOMEN

MOBY DICK

OLIVER TWIST

PETER PAN

POLLYANNA

REBECCA OF SUNNYBROOK FARM

THE SECRET GARDEN

THE TIME MACHINE

THE ADVENTURES OF
TOM SAWYER

TREASURE ISLAND

THE WIND IN THE WILLOWS

THE WONDERFUL WIZARD OF OZ

CONTENTS

CHARACTERS

JIM HAWKINS — curious lad who finds a map, joins a cruise, thinks for himself, and saves the day

JIM'S FATHER AND MOTHER — owners of the *Admiral Benbow* inn

OLD SEA DOG/"CAPTAIN"/BILLY BONES — the rough and rowdy guest at the *Admiral Benbow* inn

BLACK DOG — an old "friend" of the Old Sea Dog

OLD PEW — the blind beggar with the Black Spot

DOCTOR LIVESEY — a county doctor who puts up with no nonsense

SQUIRE TRELAWNEY — a wealthy man who puts up the money for the treasure cruise

HISPANIOLA — the ship that sets sail with twenty-seven men for Treasure Island

CHARACTERS

The Honest Men aboard the *Hispaniola*
CAPTAIN SMOLLETT — a wise and good man
JOHN HUNTER — the squire's manservant
RICHARD JOYCE — the squire's manservant
TOM REDRUTH — the squire's gameskeeper
ALAN AND TOM — refuse to join the pirates
ABRAHAM GRAY — changes to the good side

Some of the "Gentlemen of Fortune"
LONG JOHN SILVER — the crooked Sea Cook,
his shipmates call him "Barbecue"
MR. ARROW — first mate who is the first to "go"
ISRAEL HANDS — coxswain who steers the ship
DICK JOHNSON — a foolish young man
JOB ANDERSON — boatswain, captain's assistant
GEORGE MERRY — a yellow-eyed villain
TOM MORGAN — old, crafty pirate
O'BRIEN — "Redcap" who tangles with Hands

BEN GUNN — the "man of the island" marooned
for three years

CAPTAIN FLINT — Long John Silver's parrot,
named for the pirate who made the map of
Treasure Island

CHAPTER ONE

The Old Sea Dog

The Squire and the Doctor have asked me to write all I remember of Treasure Island—from the beginning to the end. I am to put everything, except where the island is located, for there is still treasure there, *not yet found*.

I will go back to the beginning, to the time when my father owned the *Admiral Benbow* inn. It was then that the brown old seaman with the scar across his cheek came to stay with us.

I remember him as if it were yesterday. He came through the inn door with a large sea chest on a cart. He was a tall, strong, heavy man, with nut-brown skin. He had a greasy black pigtail that hung down

onto his dirty blue coat. His hands were ragged with black, broken nails. And across his right cheek ran a saber-cut scar—a dirty, livid white. I remember him looking around the coastline and whistling to himself. Then he sang out in a high, cracked voice an old sea song,

> *"Fifteen men on the dead man's chest—*
> *Yo-ho-ho, and a bottle of rum!"*

He stared out at the cliffs and at our signboard. "This is a handy cove," he said to my father. "A good place for an inn. Do you have much business, mate?"

"No, not much company," replied my father, "which is a shame."

"Well, then," he said, "this is the place for me. I'm a plain man. Rum and bacon and eggs is all I want—and that room up top to watch for ships. You can just call me Captain. And you'll be wanting these—" He threw down three or four gold pieces on the table. "Tell me when I owe you more." He spoke like a man who was in charge.

His clothes were in bad shape, and he used rude language. Yet he did not seem like a regular sailor. He seemed more like a commander that was used to being obeyed and would punish—swiftly!

He was a very silent man. All day he walked around the cove or out on the cliffs with a brass telescope. All evening he sat in a corner of the parlor next to the fire and drank strong rum and water. Mostly he would not speak, even when we spoke to him. He would just give mean looks and blow through his nose like a foghorn when anyone was around. Folks that stayed at the inn soon learned to leave him alone.

Every day, when he came back from his walk, he would ask if any of us had seen any seafaring men. At first we thought he was just looking for some company and news of the sea. But when sailors *did* come to stay at the *Admiral Benbow*, he would peek through the curtain door before he would enter the parlor—and was always as quiet as a mouse around them. By then we had realized that he was indeed trying to *avoid* them.

One day he took me aside. He promised me a silver coin every month if I would only keep a secret. I was to watch and let him know if a "seafaring man with only one leg" appeared. Often, when I asked him for my silver coin each month, he would only blow through his nose at me and stare me down. Before the week was out, however,

he would pay me, and order me again to look out for "the seafaring man with one leg."

You can just imagine how that one-legged man haunted my dreams! On stormy nights, when the wind shook the house and the surf roared up the cliffs, I would picture that one-legged man. First the leg would be cut off at the knee, then at the hip. Then he was like a monster that only had the one leg—*but in the middle of his body!* To see him leap and run and chase me over hedges and creeks was the worst of nightmares.

I was terrified of this one-legged man, but everyone else at the inn was afraid of the Captain himself. He told dreadful stories about hanging, and walking the plank, and storms at sea, and wild deeds and places on the waters of the Spanish Main. If he thought someone was not listening, he would slap his hand on the table for *Silence!* His actions and his language shocked our guests.

Many a time he would sit with his rum and sing his wicked, wild sea songs. Then he would call for a round of drinks and force everyone in the room to listen to his stories or join him in a chorus. Our poor guests would tremble and join in for dear life.

My father was always saying the inn would be ruined, for people would soon stop coming by. But *I* believe that our guests rather liked him! This was fine excitement in our quiet country life. Some of the younger men called him a "true sea dog" and a "real old salt."

In one way, however, he *did* ruin us. He stayed so many months that he owed us money—and my father was too afraid to ask him for it. He lived in terror of the Captain. I'm sure this is what made my father sick and led to his early, unhappy death.

Only one time did someone cross the Captain. My father was very ill and Dr. Livesey came one evening to attend to him. Before he left, he waited in the parlor for his horse to be brought around.

How different the neat, bright doctor looked from that filthy, heavy, blurry-eyed sea dog. Suddenly the Captain began to pipe up his song:

Fifteen men on the dead man's chest—
Yo-ho-ho, and a bottle of rum!

Dr. Livesey did not seem impressed with this drunk, dirty singer. He kept talking to Taylor, the gardener. The Captain slapped his hand upon the table for *Silence!* The voices stopped at once—all but Dr. Livesey's. He went right on speaking clear and friendly. The captain glared at him, slapped his hand again, and glared still harder. Finally he roared, "Silence, there, matey!"

"You're speaking to me, sir?" said the doctor.

"Aye, matey!"

"Well, then… I have only one thing to say to you, sir," replied the doctor. "If you keep on drinking rum, you will have a stroke and the world will be rid of a very dirty scoundrel."

The Captain sprang to his feet. He pulled out and opened a sailor's clasp knife.

Dr. Livesey did not budge. He said very calmly, "Put that knife in your pocket this instant. If you do not, I promise, upon my honor, you shall hang."

The two men had a battle of looks, but the Captain soon knuckled under. He put his weapon away and sat down, grumbling like a beaten dog.

"Now, sir," said the doctor, "I'm not just a doctor. I'm a county officer. If I catch one word against you, I'll have you hunted down and forced out of this county."

Soon after, the horse arrived and Dr. Livesey rode away. The Captain held his peace that evening, and for many evenings to come.

CHAPTER TWO

Black Dog

That winter was bitter and cold, with long, hard frosts and heavy winds. My poor father was so ill that we feared he would not live to see the spring. Every day he grew worse. My mother and I had our hands full with the inn and we paid very little attention to our rough guest.

One January morning—a frosty, gray morning—the Captain got up quite early. He set out down the beach with his hat tilted back upon his head. His sword was swinging under his old blue coat and his brass telescope was under his arm. I remember that his breath hung in the air like smoke as he walked off.

Mother was upstairs with Father, and I was setting the breakfast table. The parlor door opened and a man stepped in I had never seen before. He was a pale, flabby man missing two fingers on the left hand. He wore a short sword, but he did not look much like a fighter. I was on the lookout for seafaring men (with one leg *or* two) and this one puzzled me. He did not look like a sailor, and yet he had a smack of the sea about him, too.

He sat down and asked for rum. But before I could go, he said, "Come here, sonny."

I took a step nearer.

"Is this here table for my mate Bill?" he snarled.

"I don't know a Bill," I said. "I'm setting the table for someone who goes by Captain."

"Does he have a cut on one cheek? On his right cheek? Ah, he has? Well now, is my mate Bill in this here house now?"

I told him he was out walking.

"Which way, sonny? Which way is he gone?"

I told him that the Captain would return soon.

"Ah," said he, "Bill will very happy to see me."

I did not think this would be the case. But what could I do? The stranger kept hanging about like a cat waiting for a mouse.

"Aw, here's my old mate Bill, now," he said after some time, "with a spyglass under his arm. You and me will just go back into the parlor, sonny. We'll give Bill a little surprise, we will."

The stranger backed me into the parlor and hid behind the open door. I was very uneasy and alarmed, as you may imagine. The stranger had his hand on the hilt of his sword.

At last, in walked the Captain. He slammed the door behind him and marched straight across the room to where his breakfast awaited him.

"Bill," said the stranger in a bold voice.

The Captain spun round to face us, and he turned pale. He looked as though he had seen a ghost! I felt sorry to see him look so old and sick.

"Come, Bill, you know me. You know an old shipmate, Bill, surely," said the stranger.

The captain made a sort of gasp. "Black Dog!"

"And who else?" said the man. "Black Dog, come to see his old shipmate, Billy Bones, at the *Admiral Benbow* inn. Ah, Bill, Bill, we've seen some times, us two, since I lost them two claws." He held up the hand missing the two fingers.

"Look here," said the Captain, "you've found me. Here I am. So speak up. What do you want?"

"I'll have a glass of rum from this dear child here," said Black Dog, "and we'll sit and talk over old times."

I brought in their rum, and then retreated back into the parlor. I tried hard to listen in, but I heard

only low mumbling. But at last the voices began to grow louder, and I could pick up a word or two—mostly curses from the Captain.

"No, no, no, no! And an end of it!" he cried once. "If it comes to hanging, hang all, say I."

Then all of a sudden there was a lot of noise. The chair and table went over, there was a clash of steel, and then a cry of pain! The next instant I saw Black Dog run from the inn. The Captain was right behind him. Both men had their swords drawn and Black Dog had blood running down his left shoulder.

At the door, the Captain lifted his sword for one final blow—but his sword hit our inn signboard—and there it stuck! (You can see the notch on our sign to this day.)

That blow was the last of the battle. Black Dog disappeared over the hill in half a minute.

The Captain stood staring at the signboard like a confused man. He passed his hand over his eyes a few times. Then he turned back into the house.

"Jim," he said, "bring me rum." He staggered a little, and fell against the wall.

"Are you hurt?" I cried.

"Rum," he repeated. "I must get away from here. Rum! Rum!"

I ran to fetch it, but I was very shaken. Then I heard a loud fall in the parlor. I ran back in and found the Captain lying on the floor. At the same instant my mother, who had heard all the noise, came running downstairs to help me. We raised his head. He was breathing very hard, but his eyes were closed. His face was a horrible color.

"Oh, dear!" cried my mother. "What an awful thing to happen in our house! And your poor father sick upstairs!"

We had no idea what to do to help the Captain. We were quite relieved when Doctor Livesey came in, on his visit to my father.

"Oh, Doctor," we cried, "what shall we do? Where is he wounded?"

"Wounded? Fiddlesticks!" said the doctor. "He's not wounded. The man has had a stroke— just as I warned him. Now, Mrs. Hawkins, go back upstairs to your husband, but don't tell him anything about this. I'll do my best to save this fellow's worthless life."

The doctor ripped up the Captain's sleeve to check his veins. The Captain's arm was tattooed

in several places. After a bit, the Captain opened his eyes and looked about him. First he recognized the doctor and gave him a frown. Then he looked at me. He tried to raise himself, crying, "Where's Black Dog?"

"There is no Black Dog here," said the doctor. You have had a stroke, just as I warned you. Come, now, I'll help you to your bed."

We managed to help him upstairs, and we laid him on his bed.

"Now listen to me," said the doctor. "If you keep drinking rum you'll die—do you understand that?—die."

And with that he went off to see my father, taking me with him by the arm.

"He should lie for a week where he is," he told me. "That is the best thing for him and you. But another stroke will kill him."

CHAPTER THREE

The Black Spot

About noon I stopped at the Captain's door with some cool drinks and medicine. He was still lying in bed. He seemed weak but very stirred up.

"Jim, my lad, did that doctor say how long I was to lie here?"

"A week at least," said I, walking to him.

"Thunder!" he cried. "A week! I can't do that. They'd have the Black Spot on me by then. But I'm not afraid of 'em. I'll find another place to hide, matey!"

As he spoke, he rose from bed, holding onto my shoulder. His grip almost made me cry out. Then he fell back, too weak to sit up.

"Jim, you saw that there seafaring man today?"

"Black Dog?" I asked.

"Ah! Black Dog," he said. "*He's* a bad one. But the one-legged man is worse than him. Now, if I can't get away and they give me the Black Spot, mind you, it's my old sea chest they're after. You get on a horse—you can, can't you? Well, then, you get on a horse, and go to—to that dratted doctor. You tell him to gather up officers and bring them to the *Admiral Benbow* inn. They'll find them villains here—all of Flint's old crew."

He was growing more and more excited. I was worried that he would disturb my ill father, who needed quiet.

"I was first mate," he went on. "Old Flint's first mate. I'm the only one that knows the hiding place. Flint gave it to me when he lay a-dying. But you won't tell any of this unless they put the Black Spot on me, or unless you see that Black Dog again, or a seafaring man with one leg, Jim—*him above all*."

"But what is the *Black Spot*, Captain?" I asked.

"That's an order, mate, to appear before 'em. I'll tell you if they put that on me. But you keep your eye open, Jim, and I'll share my loot with ya, upon my honor."

His voice grew weaker. After I had given him his medicine he fell into a heavy sleep. I left him, thinking about what he meant about a hiding place, the Black Spot, and Flint.

I did not think about this for long. My poor father died quite suddenly that evening, and we became lost in our sorrow. All became a blur—with visits from neighbors, planning the funeral, and taking care of the guests at the inn. I had no time to think of the Captain and his strange words.

The Captain got downstairs for breakfast the next morning, but he helped himself to rum and had a terrible temper. On the night before the funeral he was in an awful state. It was shocking, in our sad house, to hear him singing away at his ugly old sea song.

He did not speak to me, and I think he forgot what he had told me that awful night. He was very weak, but he still managed to climb the stairs. Sometimes he put his nose out of doors to smell the sea. He seemed lost in his own world, filled with fears.

So things passed until the day after the funeral. At about three o'clock on that foggy, frosty afternoon, I was standing at the door for a moment, full of sad thoughts about my father. I saw someone walking slowly beside the road. I knew he was blind, for he tapped a stick in front and wore a green shade over his eyes and nose. He was hunched over and wore a huge old tattered sea cloak with a hood. I never saw in my life a more dreadful-looking person.

He stopped in front of the inn and said, into the air, "Will some kind soul tell a poor blind man where he might be?"

"You are at the *Admiral Benbow* inn at Black Hill Cove, my good man," said I.

"I hear a voice," said he. "Will you give me your hand, my kind young friend, and lead me in?"

I held out my hand and the horrible, eyeless, soft-spoken creature gripped it hard. I was startled by the pain and tried to get free. But the blind man pulled me close up to him with a yank of his arm.

"Now, boy," he sneered, "take me in to the Captain, or I'll break your arm."

He gave my arm a wrench that made me cry out.

"Come, now, march!" he snarled.

I never heard a voice so cruel and cold and ugly as that blind man's. I led him into the parlor where the Captain was sitting, dazed with rum.

"Lead me straight up to him and cry out, 'Here's a friend for you, Bill.' If you don't, I'll wrench your arm!"

I was so terrified that I did as he told me. The poor Captain raised his eyes. His face was filled with terror and sickness. He tried to stand, but he was too weak.

"Now, Bill, sit where you are," said the blind man. "Hold out your left hand. Boy, take his left hand by the wrist and bring it near to my right."

I saw him pass something from the hand that held his stick into the Captain's palm.

"And now that's done," said the blind man. At those words he suddenly let go of me and skipped out of the parlor and into the road. I could hear his stick go tap-tap-tapping into the distance.

The Captain and I were both dazed. Then, slowly, he opened his hand and looked sharply into the palm.

"Ten o'clock!" he cried. "Six hours from now! We'll lose them yet," and he sprang to his feet. His hand went to his throat and he began swaying. He let out an odd sound—then fell straight to the floor.

I ran to him at once, calling to my mother. But it was too late. The Captain had been struck dead by a thundering stroke. I had certainly never liked the man, but as soon as I saw that he was dead, I burst into a flood of tears. It was the second death I had known, and the sorrow of the first was still fresh in my heart.

CHAPTER FOUR

The Sea Chest

I told my mother all that I knew—perhaps too late. We knew at once that we were in danger. The Captain owed us money, but we were afraid to search his room. If I rode to Doctor Livesey's for help, that would have left my mother alone and unprotected. Yet, we did not want to stay in the house. Every sound filled us with alarm—the coals falling in the kitchen grate, the very ticking of the clock. There were moments when I jumped in my skin for terror.

We decided to go forth together and seek help in the nearby village. With no head coverings, we ran out at once into the foggy night.

I was cheered to see the yellow candlelight in the windows of the village. That was the only cheer we were to feel. No soul would return with us to the *Admiral Benbow*. Several men were willing enough to ride to Dr. Livesey's, but not *one* would help us to defend the inn.

My mother made them a speech. "If none of the rest of you dare, Jim and I dare. Back we will go the way we came, and small thanks to you big, hulking, chicken-hearted men. We'll have that chest open, if we die for it. I'll have the money that's owed to us!"

Someone gave me a loaded pistol in case we were attacked. One lady let us borrow a bag for the money—if we found any. One lad was to ride to the doctor's in search of help. But that was all that came of our trip to the village.

We slipped back along the hedges, noiseless and swift. Our hearts were beating fast and we did not feel relief until the door of the *Admiral Benbow* had closed behind us.

I bolted the door at once. We stood and panted for a moment in the dark. My mother got a candle. Holding each other's hands, we went into the parlor. The Captain lay as we had left him, on his back with his eyes open and one arm stretched out.

"Pull down the blind, Jim," whispered my mother. "And then we must get the sea chest key off that—that body."

On the floor close to the Captain's hand was a little round paper, blackened on one side. It was the *Black Spot*! Written on the other side was:

"He had till ten, Mother," said I. "It's now six."

I felt in his pockets. All I found were a few small coins, a thimble, his knife, and a compass.

"Perhaps it's around his neck," said my mother.

There, sure enough, we found the key. We were filled with hope and hurried upstairs to his little room. We knelt beside his sea chest.

As my mother opened the chest, a strong smell of tobacco rose from inside. On top lay a suit of very good clothes. Next we found some sailing tools, a small tin cup, sticks of tobacco, two handsome pistols, an old Spanish watch, and five or six curious sea shells. These all lay on top of an old boat cloak, white with sea salt. Then we found the last things in the chest—a bundle of papers tied up in oilcloth, and a canvas bag that jingled of gold!

"I'll take what's owed to me and not a penny over," said my mother. "Hold the bag." She began to count out coins.

It took a while, for the coins were of different countries and sizes—doubloons, pieces of eight, and others, all together.

Suddenly I heard the tap-tapping of the blind man's stick upon the frozen road. It drew nearer and nearer while we sat holding our breath. Then it struck sharp on the inn door. We could hear the handle being turned and the bolt rattling. There was a long silence. At last the tapping started again down the road until we could hear it no more.

"Mother, take all the coins and let's be going!"

"I'll take what I have!" She jumped to her feet.

"And I'll take this to even the count," I said, picking up the oilskin packet of papers.

We left the candle by the chest and felt our way down the stairs. Then we were out the door and

running. We had not started a moment too soon. The fog was drifting off and the moon shone quite clear. Less than halfway to the village, in full moonlight, we heard footsteps running.

"My dear," said my mother weakly, "take the money and run on. I am going to faint."

Luckily, we were just at the little bridge. I helped her to the edge of the bank. Sure enough, she gave a sigh and fell on my shoulder. I do not know how I found the strength, but I managed to drag her down the bank and a little way under the arch of the bridge. So there we had to stay—partly hidden and within earshot of the inn.

My curiosity was stronger than my fear. I crept back up and could see the road and our door. There I saw seven or eight men running hard. *Pirates!* I thought. A man with a lantern led the way. The next moment I heard the blind man's voice cry, "Down with the door!"

"Aye, aye, sir!" answered two or three. A rush was made upon the door, and they were surprised to find it unlocked.

Again the blind man's voice rang out, as if he were afire with rage, "In, in, in!"

A few dashed in. One called out, "Bill's dead."

"Search him, you lazy lubbers, and the rest of you get the chest."

I could hear their feet rattling up our stairs. The house must have shook with it. The upstairs window of the Captain's room was thrown open and a man leaned out.

"Pew," he cried, "someone's been in the chest."

"Is it there?" roared Pew.

"The money's there."

"Forget the money! Flint's papers, I mean!"

"We don't see it here," replied the man.

"It's that boy. I wish I had put his eyes out!" cried blind Pew. "Scatter, lads, and find 'em."

I could hear the sounds of the house being searched and torn apart. Then from over the hill came a distant whistle.

"There's the signal," said one. "We'll have to move, mates."

"Move, my eye!" cried Pew. "That boy can't be far! Scatter and look, dogs! Oh, shiver my soul," he cried, "if I had eyes!"

"Hang it, Pew, we've *got* the gold!" growled one.

"They might have hid the thing," said another. "Take the gold, Pew. Don't stand here storming."

While they quarreled, another sound came from the top of the hill—the tramp of horses galloping and a pistol shot! The pirates turned at once and ran in every direction. No one remained but Pew, tapping up and down the road, calling out, "Johnny, Black Dog, Dirk! You won't leave old Pew, mates—not old Pew!"

Just then four or five riders swept at full gallop down the hill. Pew turned with a scream and rolled into the ditch. He was on his feet again in a second and made another dash. But he was so confused, he ran and fell right under the nearest horse. The rider tried to save him, but it was too late. Down went Pew with a cry that rang high into the night.

He fell on his side, then gently rolled face down and moved no more.

I called out and soon saw who the riders were. One was the boy who had gone from the village to Dr. Livesey's. The rest were officers on their way to investigate a ship docked in Kitt's Hole.

Pew was dead, stone dead. As for my mother, we carried her up to the village. A little cold water and smelling salts soon brought her back again.

I told the whole story to Chief Officer Dance. I went back with him to the *Admiral Benbow* and found it in a state of smash. I could see at once that we were ruined.

"They got the money, you say? Well, then, Hawkins, what were they after? More money?"

"No, sir, not money, I think. In fact, sir, I believe I have the thing in my pocket. And to tell you the truth, I would like to get it somewhere safe... To Doctor Livesey's, I thought..."

"To be sure, boy. Quite right," said he. "And I should report Mister Pew's death to Dr. Livesey or Squire Trelawney. I'll take you along."

I thanked him and we walked back to the village where the horses were. I told my mother where I was off to. Then I got up behind one of the officers and we began down the road to Dr. Livesey's.

CHAPTER FIVE

The Treasure Map

When we reached Dr. Livesey's, the maid told us that the doctor had gone to Squire Trelawney's to dine. We rode to the grounds of the squire and were admitted warmly at the grand Hall. A servant led us into the library where the two men sat on either side of a bright fire. The squire was a tall, stout man, over six feet high. He had a rough-n-ready face and a look that said he was better than others—or *thought* he was.

"Come in, Mr. Dance," he said.

"Good evening, Mr. Dance," said the doctor with a nod. "And good evening to you, friend Jim. What good wind brings you here?"

Mr. Dance stood up straight and stiff and told the entire story. The two men hung on every word. When they heard how my mother went back to the inn, the squire cried, "Bravo!"

"And so, Jim," said the doctor, "you have the thing that these pirates were after, have you?"

"Here it is, sir," said I, and gave him the packet.

The doctor looked it all over, as if his fingers were itching to open it. Then he put it quietly in the pocket of his coat.

"Squire," said he, "Mr. Dance, of course, must be off to his duties. I will keep Jim Hawkins here to sleep at my house. But first he must eat."

A cold meat pie was brought in and I had a hearty supper, for I was as hungry as a hawk. While I ate, the squire and the doctor bid farewell to Mr. Dance and closed the door behind him.

"And now, squire," said the doctor.

"And now, Livesey," said the squire in the same breath.

"One at a time, one at a time," laughed Dr. Livesey. "You have heard of this Flint, I suppose?"

"Heard of him!" cried the squire. "He was the most blood-thirsty pirate that sailed. Blackbeard was a *child* compared to Flint."

"But did he have any money?" asked the doctor.

"Money!" cried the squire. "That's all these villains lived for!"

"Suppose that I have here in my pocket some clue to where Flint buried his treasure. Will that treasure amount to much?"

"Amount, sir!" cried the squire. "It would amount to this: If we have the clue you talk about, I'll get a ship ready in Bristol dock. I'll take you and Hawkins here along, and I'll have that treasure if I search a year."

"Very well," said the doctor. "Now then, if Jim agrees to it, we'll open the packet." He laid it before him on the table.

The bundle was sewn together, and the doctor cut the stitches with his medical scissors. It contained two things—a book and a sealed paper.

"First of all we'll try the book," said the doctor.

The squire and I peered over his shoulder as the doctor went through the book. It was filled with nearly twenty years of notes, dates and strange markings. Here and there was a sum of money along with several crosses and place names. Under the sum on the last page was written: "Bones, his pile."

"I can't make head or tail of this," said the doctor.

"The thing is as clear as noonday," cried the squire. "This is an account book. These crosses stand for the names of ships or towns that they sank or plundered. The added up figures are the scoundrel's share."

"Right you are, I believe!" said the doctor. "A thrifty man! Not one to be cheated."

"And now," said the squire, "for the other."

The paper had been sealed in several places. The doctor opened the seals with great care, and there fell out the map of an island. It was clearly marked with latitude and longitude, water depth, names of hills and bays and inlets—everything that would be needed to find it and safely anchor a ship there. It was about nine miles long and five across. It had two fine harbors and a hill in the center part marked "Spyglass Hill." There were three X's marked in red—two on the north part of the island, one in the southwest. Next to this last X were the words:

BULK OF TREASURE

Over on the back was written:

Tall tree, Spyglass shoulder,
bearing a point to the N. of N.N.E.
Skeleton Island E.S.E. and by E.   Ten feet.

The silver bars are in the north spot. Near the east hill,
ten fathoms south of the black crag with the face on it.

The weapons are easy to find, in the sandhill,
N. point of north inlet cape, bearing E. and a quarter N.
                                            —J .Flint

That was all. But it filled both men with delight.

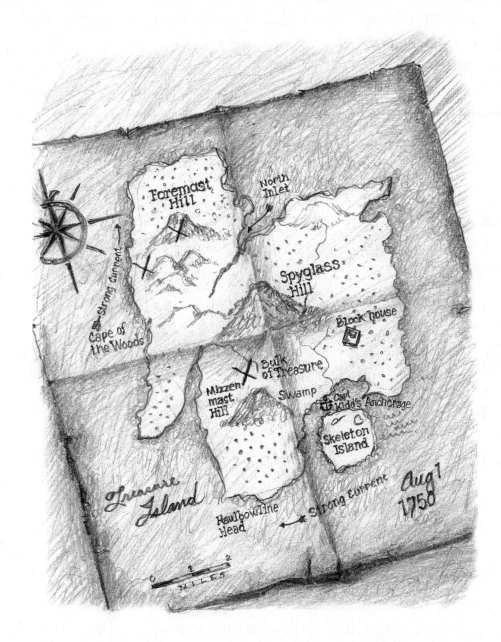

"Livesey," said the squire, "you will give up your medical practice at once. Tomorrow I start for Bristol. In three weeks' time—three weeks!—two weeks—ten days—we'll have the best ship, sir, and the choicest crew in England. Hawkins shall come as cabin boy. You, Livesey, are ship's doctor. I am admiral. We'll take my servants—Redruth, Joyce, and Hunter. We'll have a quick passage and no trouble finding the spot. And we'll have money to eat—to *roll* in—to play with ever after."

"Trelawney," said the doctor, "I'll go with you. So will Jim. There's only *one* man I'm afraid of."

"And who's that?" cried the squire. "Name the dog, sir!"

"You," replied the doctor, "for you cannot hold your tongue. We are not the only men who know of this map. These fellows who attacked the inn are after this map and the treasures. None of us should be alone until we get to sea. Jim and I shall stick together in the meanwhile. You'll take Joyce and Hunter when you ride to Bristol. And from first to last, not *one* of us must breathe a word of what we've found."

"Livesey," returned the squire, "you are always right. I promise—I'll be as silent as the grave."

I lived on at the squire's Hall with Tom Redruth, the squire's gamekeeper. Squire Trelawney was hard at work in Bristol finding a ship and a crew. Doctor Livesey had to go to London to find a doctor to take his place in the village. This all took longer than we had planned, and I often felt like a prisoner with old Redruth.

My days were full of sea dreams of strange islands and adventures. I thought about all the markings I could remember from the map. I would sit by the fire and picture that island. In my mind I explored every part and climbed the tall hill called the Spyglass. Sometimes we fought with savages. Sometimes dangerous animals hunted us. (But nothing I could dream up would ever be as strange or as awful as what our real adventures turned out to be!)

So the weeks passed on, till one fine day there came a letter from the squire! Redruth opened it and read it aloud. The squire had found a ship called the *Hispaniola*. She was at anchor, ready to sail. She weighed two hundred tons! He wrote that his friend Mr. Blandly was very excited about our hunt for treasure.

"Oh, no," I said. "The squire has been talking."

The letter went on to say that he had hired a sea cook. His name was Long John Silver, and he had lost a leg while serving in the Royal Navy. This cook helped him find a good, tough crew of "old salts." Mr. Blandly found us a captain—a stiff man, but a good man. And Long John Silver found a first mate for us by the name of Mr. Arrow. The good ship *Hispaniola* was ready to sail!

A few final notes: I was to go with Redruth and spend one night with my mother to say good-bye. Then we were all to come as soon as we could. Lastly, Mr. Blandly promised to send a search party if our ship did not return by August.

Imagine my excitement! The next morning Redruth and I set out for the *Admiral Benbow*. My mother was in good health and glad to see me. The inn had been repaired and painted—thanks to the squire. He had even hired a boy to help my mother while I was gone—and this made me realize that I was truly going away. I had a few tears.

The next day, I said good-bye to my mother and the cove where I had lived all my life. I thought of the old Captain—how he had walked this beach with his drooping hat and his brass spyglass. Then we were on our way.

CHAPTER SIX

Long John Silver

I dozed off in the coach. When I awoke, the day was breaking and we were in a large city—Bristol!

We got out and walked down the street toward the docks where Mr. Trelawney was staying at an inn. We saw ships of all sizes and nations! Sailors were singing, some were high overhead on ropes that looked like spider threads. I had lived by the shore all my life, but now I was truly near the sea! The smell of tar and salt was something new. I saw the most wonderful ships that had sailed the oceans. I saw old sailors with rings in their ears, and whiskers curled in ringlets, and pigtails. This was grander than seeing kings!

And I was going to sea myself—to sea in the *Hispaniola*, with pigtailed singing sailors! To sea, bound for an unknown island, and to seek for buried treasure!

We came in front of a large inn and met Squire Trelawney, who was all smiles. He was dressed in blue like a sea officer.

"Here you are," he cried, "and the doctor came last night from London. Bravo! The ship's crew is complete!"

"Oh, sir," cried I, "when do we sail?"

"Sail!" says he. "We sail tomorrow!"

After breakfast, the squire gave me a note to take to Long John Silver. He said I would easily find his tavern, the *Spyglass*, along the docks. It had a large brass telescope for a sign. I set off, overjoyed to see some more of the ships and sailors. I made my way among a great crowd of people and carts, for the dock was now at its busiest, until I found the *Spyglass* tavern.

It was a clean, bright little place with neat red curtains and an open door. Inside were mostly seafaring men. They talked so loudly that I was almost afraid to enter.

Then I saw a man come out of a side room. I was sure he must be Long John. His left leg was cut off close by the hip. Under the left shoulder he carried a crutch. He did well with this crutch, cheerfully hopping about upon it like a bird as he moved among the tables. He was very tall and strong, with a face as big as a ham—plain and pale, but intelligent and smiling. He whistled and merrily gave a hearty slap on the shoulder to a few guests.

Now, to tell you the truth, when I first heard of Long John Silver, I was afraid that he might be that one-legged man whom the Captain feared. But now I knew this could not be that man. I knew what a pirate looked like. I had seen the Captain, and Black Dog, and blind Pew. This Long John Silver was pleasant and jolly—unlike those other miserable scoundrels.

I plucked up courage at once and walked right up to the man.

"Mr. Silver, sir?" I asked, holding out the note.

"Yes, my lad," said he. "Such is my name, to be sure. And who may you be?" Then he looked at the squire's letter and said, quite loudly, "Oh! I see. You are our new cabin boy. Pleased I am to see you."

I shook his large firm hand.

Just then one of the men at a back table rose and ran for the door. I noticed him and recognized him at once. It was the man missing two fingers who had first come to the *Admiral Benbow*.

"Oh," I cried, "stop him! It's Black Dog!"

"I don't care two coppers who he is," cried Silver. "He hasn't paid! Harry, run and catch him."

One of the men near the door leaped up and ran after him.

"Who did you say he was?" asked Silver. "Black what?"

"Dog, sir," said I. "Didn't Squire Trelawney tell you about the pirates? That man was one of them."

"That so?" cried Silver. "In my house! Ben, run and help Harry. One of those pirates, was he? Was that you sitting with him, Morgan? Step up here."

Morgan, an old, gray-haired, dark-faced sailor, came slowly forward.

"Now, Morgan," said Silver very sternly, "you never set eyes on that… er… Black Dog before, did you, now?"

"Not I, sir," said Morgan with a salute.

"You didn't know his name, did you?"

"No, sir."

"Get back to your seat, then. Well, let's see— Black Dog? No, I don't know the name, not I.

Yet I kind of think I've—yes, I've seen him. He used to come here with a blind beggar, he did."

"I knew that blind man, too," I said. "His name was Pew."

"It was!" cried Silver. "Pew! That were his name for certain. Ah, he looked a shark, he did! But Ben will run that Black Dog down!"

Silver went stumping up and down the tavern on his crutch, slapping tables with his hand. I began again to wonder about this man. After all… I had seen Black Dog in his tavern!

The men came back—with no Black Dog. Silver was very upset.

"See here, Hawkins," he said, "what will Cap'n Trelawney think? Me with a pirate in my tavern? But I see you're a smart lad—smart as paint. You saw that we tried to catch 'im. Why, shiver my timbers, what could *I* do on this one leg of mine? I'll walk along with you and tell Trelawney the story."

On our little walk to the inn along the docks, Silver told me interesting things about the different boats. He knew all about where they were going and what they were loading. He told me stories and taught me seafaring words and phrases. He was one of the best shipmates a lad could hope for!

When we got to the inn, the squire and Dr. Livesey were seated together. Long John told the story of Black Dog in his tavern.

"That was how it were, now, weren't it, Hawkins?" he said, now and again.

The squire and the doctor both agreed that there was nothing more to be done about it. Long John took up his crutch and hobbled out the door.

"All hands on deck by four this afternoon," shouted the squire after him.

"Aye, aye, sir," cried the sea cook.

"Well, squire," said Dr. Livesey, "this John Silver suits me."

"The man's a good sort," said the squire. "And now, Hawkins, take your hat and we'll see the ship!"

CHAPTER SEVEN

We Set Sail

The *Hispaniola* lay some way out. As we stepped aboard we were met and saluted by the first mate, Mr. Arrow. He was a brown old sailor with earrings in his ears and a squint. He and Squire Trelawney were very friendly, but the squire did *not* like our ship's captain, Captain Smollett.

Our captain was a sharp-looking man who seemed angry with everything on board. In a private meeting with the squire, the doctor and me, the captain let us know his views.

"I don't like this cruise. I don't like the men. And I don't like my officer, Mr. Arrow. And there it is," the captain said.

He went on to say that he should have selected his own men. And did not like the rumors he was hearing from the sailors—that this was a voyage in search of treasure—with a pirate's map to follow.

"I never told that to a soul," cried the squire.

"The men know it, sir," said the captain. "I don't know who has this map. But I want it kept secret. From me and from the crew—and from the first mate, Mr. Arrow."

"You don't like Mr. Arrow?" asked the doctor.

"He's too friendly with the crew. And he stumbles about—I fear he drinks, sir. I am responsible for the ship's safety and the life of every man aboard of her. I *will* speak up when I fear trouble, for 'tis my duty, sir. Treasure cruises are never safe—*sir.*"

And with that he took his leave.

"Trelawney," said the doctor, "I believe you have two honest men on board with you—that captain and John Silver."

"Silver, if you like," cried the squire, "but not that captain! He does not set well by me!"

"Well," said the doctor, "we shall see. We shall see."

All that night we hustled about loading and getting the ship ready to sail. I was dog tired. A little before dawn, the sailor sounded his pipe and the crew began to man the capstan bars—which means they started to bring up the anchor.

"Now, Barbecue, give us a tune," cried one voice.

"The old tune," cried another.

"Aye, aye, mates," said Long John, who was standing by, with his crutch under his arm. At once he sang out the tune and words I knew so well:

Fifteen men on the dead man's chest—

And then the whole crew joined in—

Yo-ho-ho, and a bottle of rum!

And at the last "Ho!" they all pushed on the capstan bars, hauling the anchor up a little more each time.

Soon the anchor was up and the sails began to fill. The *Hispaniola* had begun her voyage to the Isle of Treasure.

The ship proved to be a good ship. The crew were able seamen. And the captain understood his business. But before we got to Treasure Island, two or three things happened which I must record and make known.

Mr. Arrow, first of all, turned out even worse than the captain had feared. No one listened to his orders. He was clumsy and sloppy, and it was thought he must be drunk. Nobody was surprised when one dark night he disappeared and was seen no more.

"Overboard!" said the captain, shaking his head.

Job Anderson was named new first mate. He watched our course and helped the captain. And the coxswain—the man who steered the ship—was Israel Hands. He was a wily, old, experienced sailor who could be trusted with almost anything.

But my favorite of them all was Long John Silver. He was a good sea cook and the men called him Barbecue. He carried his crutch by a rope round his neck. This way, both hands were free for cooking. He kept his cook's galley as clean as a new pin. The dishes were always hanging up. In one corner was his parrot in a cage.

"He's no common man, that Barbecue," said the coxswain to me. "He's as brave as a lion. I seen him grapple four men and knock their heads together."

All the crew respected and even obeyed Long John Silver. He had a way of helping each man in some special way.

Long John Silver was always kind to me and always glad to see me in the cook's galley.

"Come away, Hawkins," he would say. "Come and have a yarn with John. You're young, you are, but you're as smart as paint. I seen that when I set my eyes on you. I can talk to you like a man, my son. Sit you down and hear the news. Here's Cap'n Flint—I calls my parrot Cap'n Flint, after the famous buccaneer. Cap'n Flint was just sayin' our voyage will be a success. Wasn't you, cap'n?"

And the parrot would say, very quickly, "Pieces of eight! Pieces of eight! Pieces of eight!"

"Now, that bird," he would say, "is maybe two hundred years old, Hawkins. They live forever, mostly. She's sailed with pirates, she has. She's been to Madagascar, and Malabar, and Portobello. That's how she learned 'Pieces of eight.' You've seen a might of gold in your time, ain't ya, cap'n?"

"Stand by to go about," the parrot would scream.

The squire and Captain Smollett did not speak to each other much. The squire despised the captain. The captain admitted he liked the ship once it had set sail. Still he muttered, "But I don't like the cruise."

CHAPTER EIGHT

What I Heard in the Apple Barrel

Every man on board seemed well content. And never was a ship's company so spoiled. Double grog was often served and there was plum-pudding every few days. Plus we always had a huge barrel of apples on deck for anyone to help himself.

"Spoil the hands and ye make devils. That's my belief," the captain said to Dr. Livesey. "Never knew good come of it yet."

But good *did* come of the apple barrel, as you shall hear. For if it had not been for that, we might have all perished.

This was how it came about.

It was about the last day of our voyage. We were

expecting to see Treasure Island late that night or early next day. The *Hispaniola* rolled steadily. Everyone was in the bravest spirits because we were now so near an end of the first part of our adventure.

Now, just after sundown, when all my work was over, I decided to have an apple. The huge apple barrel was nearly empty, so I just crawled over and into the barrel. I sat right down inside to enjoy an apple. I was so tired that the sound of the waters and the rocking movement of the ship put me nearly to sleep.

I was jolted awake when a heavy man sat down close by. The barrel shook as he leaned his shoulders against it. I was just about to jump up when the man began to speak. It was Silver's voice. Before I had heard a dozen words, I would not have shown myself for all the world. Instead I lay there, trembling and listening. Just from Silver's first few words, I realized that all the honest men on board were in danger!

What I heard that night in the apple barrel chilled me to the bone! Long John Silver was telling one of the young sailors, Dick, about his *pirating days!*

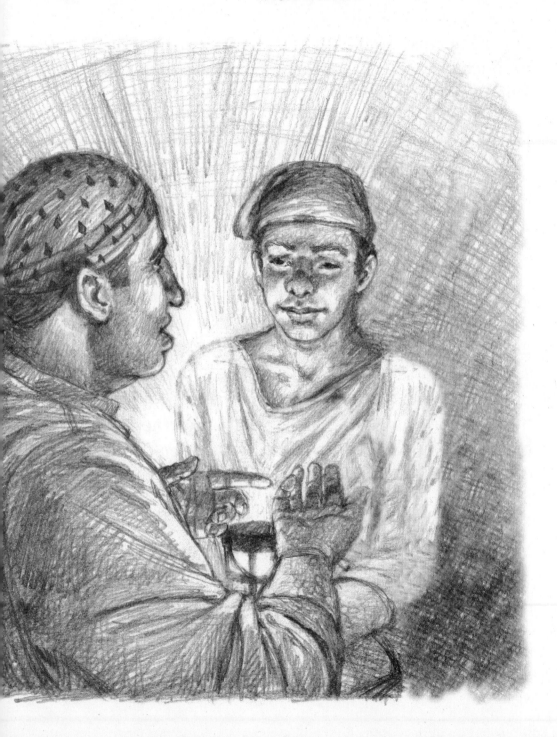

"Flint was cap'n," he said, "It was on the same plunder that old Pew lost his eyes that I lost this leg. But we got a lot of gold, we did!"

"Ah!" cried the young sailor, "I hear he was the best, was Flint!"

Long John Silver went on to brag about his adventures. He said that most of Flint's old men were here—on the *Hispaniola!* He was trying to get poor Dick to join the pirates.

"You look here," Silver said, "you're young, you are, but you're as smart as paint. I seen that when I set my eyes on you. I'll talk to you like a man."

You may imagine how I felt. These were the same words the villain had said to me.

"You'd make a fine gentleman of fortune, Dick," Silver went on. "They lives rough, and they risk hanging from the gallows. But they get gold, they do—pounds and pounds of it. Ah, you may be sure of gettin' rich on old John's ship."

"Well," replied Dick, "I didn't like the idea till I had this talk with you, John, but here's my hand."

"And a brave lad you are," answered Silver. They shook hands so heartily that the barrel shook. "And a finer gentleman of fortune I never clapped my eyes on."

By this time I understood that a "gentleman of fortune" was just a common pirate. Silver had Dick on his side, now! Silver gave a little whistle and a third man strolled up and sat down.

"Dick is with us," said Silver.

"Oh, I know'd Dick was smart," returned a voice. It was Israel Hands. "He's no fool. When are we gonna do 'em in, Barbecue?"

"Here's the plan, men," said Silver. "They've got the map. So we'll let this squire and doctor find the stuff and get it aboard. Then we'll finish with 'em at the island."

"But," asked Dick, "shouldn't we just leave 'em on the island?"

"Put 'em ashore and maroon 'em?" said the sea cook rascal. "Or cut 'em down?"

"Dead men don't bite," said Israel Hands.

"Right you are," said Silver. "I give my vote—death. Wait is what I say. But when the time comes, why, let her rip! But I claim Trelawney. He's mine!" Then he added in a cheery voice, "Dick, jump up, like a sweet lad, and get me an apple!"

Imagine my terror! I heard Dick begin to rise—and then, almost at the same time, the voice of the lookout shouted, "Land ho!"

There was a great rush of feet across the deck. I slipped out of that apple barrel and dived behind the fore-sail. No one had noticed! I ran for the open deck to look for the squire and the doctor.

Everyone was staring out to sea. We saw an island with two low hills and a third and higher hill. The highest peak was buried in the fog. I heard Captain Smollett giving orders. It all seemed like a foggy dream, for I was still in terror from what I had just overheard.

"And now, men," said the captain, "has any one of you ever seen that land ahead?"

"I have, sir," said Silver. "When I was a cook for a trader ship. That hill to the north they calls the Foremast Hill. The far south hill is Mizzenmast Hill. The highest in the middle they calls Spyglass Hill. There's a harbor just round it with a small island. Skeleton Island they calls it—in the harbor cove."

"Thank you, my man," said Captain Smollett. "I'll ask you later on to give us a help. You may go."

I was surprised at how coolly John told of the island. A shudder went through when he laid his hand upon my arm.

"Ah," says he, "this here is a sweet spot, this island—a sweet spot for a lad to get ashore on. You'll bathe, and you'll climb trees, and you'll hunt goats, you will. Why, it makes me young again. When you want to do a bit of exploring, you just ask ol' John, and he'll give ya snacks to take along."

I found Captain Smollett, the squire, and Dr. Livesey talking together on the quarter-deck. I whispered to the doctor, "Bring the captain and squire down to the cabin. I have terrible news."

In the cabin the squire said, "Now, Hawkins, you have something to say. Speak up."

I told the whole details of Silver's plans. Nobody interrupted me. They kept their eyes upon my face from first to last.

"Well, gentlemen," said the captain, "We can't turn back. We must keep a bright lookout. The map shows a stockade with a blockhouse near the harbor. We'll hole up there and do our planning. We have the four of us plus Trelawney's home servants—Redruth, Hunter and Joyce. That makes seven against their nineteen—and there may be more that come to our side."

"Jim here," said the doctor, "can help us more than anyone. The men are friendly with him. Jim is a noticing lad."

"Hawkins, I put great faith in you," added Squire Trelawney.

Only seven against nineteen. And one of these seven was me—a boy!

CHAPTER NINE

My Shore Adventure

The next morning I hurried on deck to see the island. I could see its three wooded hills and the yellow sand on the beach. Still, to me the island looked gray and sad. From that first look, I hated the very thought of Treasure Island.

All the way in, Long John stood by the man at the wheel and directed the ship. He knew the passage like the palm of his hand. We sailed three or four miles round the corner of the island and came up into a passage into a natural harbor. The main island lay to one side and the small Skeleton Island was on the other. We dropped anchor in the same spot that had been marked on our map.

The shoreline looked flat and led into woods. Two little swampy rivers emptied into this cove. From the ship we could not see the stockade or blockhouse which were marked on the map. The cove had a rotten odor. I saw the doctor sniffing and sniffing, like someone tasting a bad egg.

"I don't know about treasure," he said, "but I'll bet my wig there's fever here. It smells of malaria."

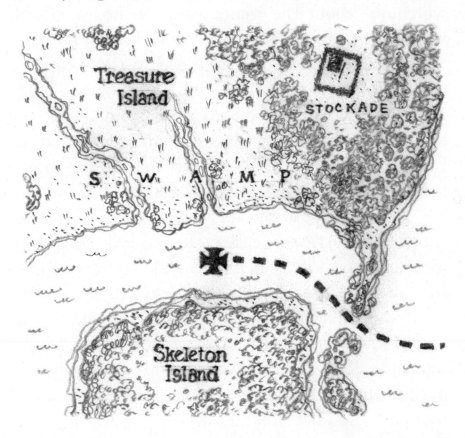

We had much work, for the little jolly-boats had to be loaded. The men grumbled over their work in the hot sun. Anderson was in charge of the boat I worked on, and he grumbled the loudest. The crew was edgy and itching to get ashore.

The captain called a private meeting in his cabin. He had decided to let the grumpy crew have an afternoon on shore. Hunter, Joyce and Redruth were told about the pirate gang on board. Pistols were handed out to the seven of us honest men.

When the captain announced to the crew that they could take the jolly-boats to shore, they cheered. The cheer echoed off the hills and sent the birds flying and squawking around the harbor. I believe the silly fellows must have thought they'd find treasure the minute they landed.

As soon as the captain was in his cabin, Silver sneakily took over as leader. He gathered up twelve men to go to shore with him. Six of the crew were to stay on the ship—along with our seven.

It was then that I had my first wild idea (which ended up saving our lives). I decided to slip ashore, too! In a jiffy I slipped over the side and curled up in the front of the nearest boat. Almost at the same moment, the boat shoved off.

No one noticed me but the man at the oar. "Is that you, Jim? Keep your head down." But Silver looked sharply over from his boat. "Is that Jim there?" he called. I began to regret what I had done.

My boat was the first to come along the wooded part of the shore. I caught hold of a tree branch as we passed by, swung myself out, and plunged into the bushes while Silver and the rest were still a ways behind.

"Jim, Jim!" I heard Silver shouting.

As you can guess, I didn't answer! I ran, jumped, and ducked through the bushes until I could run no longer. I had given the slip to Long John Silver! Now I could explore this strange land.

I found swamps and also a sandy area with a few pine trees. I could see one of the hills, with two craggy peaks shining in the sun.

I was truly on my own! No one lived on the island. My shipmates were far behind me, and I was free! I saw strange flowers and snakes. One raised his head from a rock and hissed at me with a noise that sounded like a rattle.

One area had small twisted oaks that grew in clumps. I followed these oaks till I came to one of the little rivers that emptied into the swampy cove. The swamp was steaming in the strong sun. I could see Spyglass Hill through the haze.

Suddenly I heard two voices—and one was Long John Silver's. I crawled into the tangle of the small oaks, silent as a mouse. Peeking through the leaves, I could see down beside the swamp. There was Silver talking to Tom, a crewman, in the hot sun. I could hear Silver trying to get Tom to join the side of the pirates, and Tom was not in agreement.

"Silver," said Tom, "I won't join that mess of swabs. I'd sooner lose my hand. If I turn against my duty—"

Tom was interrupted by a cry of anger that came from far out in the marsh. Then came one long, horrid scream. The rocks of Spyglass Hill made the scream echo over the island. Birds rose in the air. It was a scream of death—and it was ringing in my brain.

Tom was startled by the scream, but Silver just rested on his crutch, watching Tom like a snake about to spring.

"John! In heaven's name, who was that?"

"That?" Silver smiled calmly. "Oh, I reckon that was Alan."

"Alan!" Tom cried. "Rest his soul. John Silver, you're no mate of mine. If I die like a dog, I'll die doing my duty. You've killed Alan, have you? Kill me, too, if you can. But I won't join you."

And with that, this brave fellow began to walk away. Silver grabbed the branch of a tree, whipped the crutch out of his armpit, and threw it like a spear. It struck poor Tom right between the shoulders in the middle of his back. His hands flew up, he gave a sort of gasp, and fell down.

The whole world seemed to swirl around me as I fainted from shock. When I came to, the monster had his crutch back under his arm. Tom lay on the ground, dead. I could not believe a human life had been cut short so cruelly before my eyes.

Silver then blew upon a whistle. I instantly got out of my hiding spot and headed toward the woods. I could hear calls between Silver and the other pirates. I ran as I never ran before, full of fear. It was all over, I thought. Good-bye to the *Hispaniola*. Good-bye to the squire, the doctor, and the captain!

I was still running when I came to the little hill with the two peaks. The air was fresh here, and I stopped to breathe deeply.

But here a fresh scare started my heart thumping even more!

CHAPTER TEN

The Man of the Island

I saw something dark and shaggy slip behind the trunk of a pine tree. Filled with this new terror, I started to run back the way I had come.

But the figure kept up with me, leaping like a deer between the tree trunks. Somehow, I found the courage to stop and face this strange animal.

It must have been watching me. It stepped out from behind the tree, hid again, then stepped out again and fell to his knees. It was a man!

"Who are you?" I asked.

"Ben Gunn," he answered in a cracked voice that sounded like a rusty lock. "I'm poor Ben Gunn, I am. I haven't spoke with a man these three years."

He was an odd sight! His skin was burnt by the sun, and even his lips were black. He was the most ragged man I had ever seen. His clothes were made from old tattered ship sails and goatskins. A brass-buckled leather belt, leather strings, brass buttons, and bits of stick held his outfit together.

"Three years!" I cried. "Were you shipwrecked?"

"Nay, mate," said he. "I were marooned."

Marooned! I knew the word. This meant he had been left alone on the island as a punishment.

"Marooned three years ago," he said, as he felt my jacket and looked at my boots. "I lived on goats, and berries, and oysters. But, mate, my heart is sore for some tasty food. Do you happen to have a piece of cheese about you, now? No? Well, many nights I've dreamed of cheese—toasted, mostly..."

"If ever I can get aboard the ship again," I said, "you shall have cheese by the pound."

"If ever you can get aboard again, eh?" he repeated. "Why, now, Ben Gunn can help you there... er... what do you call yourself, mate?"

"Jim," I told him.

"Well, Jim," he whispered, "I'm rich."

I now felt sure that the poor fellow had gone crazy alone on this island.

"Rich! Rich! I say," he went on. "You'll bless your stars, Jim, that you was the first to find me!"

He gripped my hand tighter and raised a finger.

"Now, Jim, you tell me true. That ain't Flint's ship, is it?" he asked.

"It's not Flint's ship, and Flint is dead. But there are some of Flint's men aboard."

"Not a man—with one—leg?" he gasped.

"Silver?" I asked.

"Ah, Silver!" says he. "That were his name."

"He's the cook, and the ringleader, too." I told him the whole story of our voyage and the pirates. When I had told him all, he patted me on the head.

"You're a good lad, Jim," he said, "and you're all in a knot of trouble, ain't you? Well, you can trust Ben Gunn. Would your squire be needin' help from a man with, say, one thousand pounds of money?"

"I am sure he would," said I.

"And would he give that man a way home?" he added, with a sharp eye.

"The squire's a gentleman," I cried. "He'll take you. Besides, you could help us sail the ship home."

"So I could, Jim. Now, I'll tell you my story," he said. "I were in Flint's ship when he buried the treasure—he and six strong sailors. They was ashore for a week. Me and Billy Bones and John Silver stayed aboard our ship, the *Walrus*. One fine day, here come Flint by himself in a little boat. And wheer were the other six? Murdered and buried. And wheer was the treasure? Buried—on the island!

"Well, three years ago I was in another ship, and we sailed near this island. 'Boys,' said I, 'here's Flint's treasure. Let's land and find it.' Twelve days we looked for it, but found nothing. My mates were so angry with me that they sailed off—without me.

"Well, Jim, three years have I been here. You tell the squire this. I spend some time in prayers. I spend other times thinkin' about my dear mother. But most of my time was took up with another matter. And then you'll give the squire a pinch, like this." He winked at me and pinched my arm.

"Well," I said, "I don't know what you mean, but it doesn't matter. We don't have a way to get on board the ship, and the pirates are sure to take it."

"Ah," said he, "that's the hitch. Well, I've made me a boat with my two hands. I keep her under the large white rock. We might try that after dark."

And just then, the island echoed with the thunder of cannon fire.

"Hi!" he cried. "What's that?"

"That's the cannon on the ship! They have begun to fight!" I cried. "Follow me."

I ran toward the cove. The goatskin man trotted along, saying as we ran, "Keep to your left, mate! Under the trees! Theer's wheer I killed my first goat. Ah! And theer's the cemetery. I come here and prays when I think a Sunday is due."

Next we heard gun fire. Then up ahead I saw the Union Jack, our British flag, flutter in the air above the high picket fence of a stockade.

When Ben Gunn saw the flag he stopped and sat down. "Theer's your friends, sure enough," he said.

"Or the pirates," I answered.

"Nay! Silver flies the Jolly Roger with the skull and crossbones. Theer's been fighting, and your friends are in the stockade Flint made years ago."

"Well," said I, "let's hurry on and join them."

"Nay, mate," said Ben, "not till I see your squire and has his word that he'll help me. And when you want Ben Gunn, you know wheer to find him. Just wheer you found him today. And, Jim, if you see Silver, you wouldn't tell on Ben Gunn, would you?"

Then came another loud boom. A cannonball tore through the trees and landed in the sand near us. We took off running in different directions.

For an hour the boom of the cannon shook the island and balls kept crashing through the woods. I moved toward the cove, staying away from the stockade where the cannonballs were aimed.

The sun had just set. A cold sea breeze was ruffling the gray water. The tide was out, and a sandy area led to Skeleton Island across the cove. The *Hispaniola* was still anchored, *but she was flying the Jolly Roger!* I knew then that my friends were inside the stockade. I must get back to it.

As I rose to my feet, I saw a huge white rock out on the sandy area toward Skeleton Island. Could this be the white rock that Ben Gunn had spoken of? Where he said he had hidden a boat? I kept this in mind as I made my way through the woods.

I reached the stockade and climbed over the tall picket fence. I landed inside and saw my faithful friends as they ran over to joyfully greet me.

But it was also a sad greeting, for not *all* my friends were there. I learned that old Thomas Redruth had been killed.

The doctor led me to the blockhouse and told me what had happened.

CHAPTER ELEVEN

Inside the Stockade

After the pirates had taken the two jolly-boats to shore, the doctor, the squire and the captain had met in the cabin. They knew that the pirates could take the ship at any time. So, they decided to attack the six pirates on board, pull up anchor, and sail away. Then Hunter came in and said, "Jim Hawkins has gone ashore." So the plans changed.

The doctor and Hunter quietly took a jolly-boat to shore and found their way to the stockade which was drawn on the map. They climbed over the six-foot-high fence. Inside the area was a blockhouse built over a cool spring of fresh water. This was the best place to defend against any attack.

They returned to the ship in the jolly-boat, and went into action. They loaded the boat with food and weapons to take back to the stockade. Joyce, Hunter, and the doctor made this second trip. Joyce and Hunter stayed to guard the stockade. The doctor oared back to the ship for yet a third trip to bring the rest of the good men to shore.

The captain had called out to the pirates on board asking who would switch to their good side. "I give you thirty seconds to answer me," he cried.

At this, Abraham Gray broke away from the pirates and, with a slashed cheek, dashed to the jolly-boat. Then these five men—the captain, the squire, the doctor, Gray, and Redruth—left the *Hispaniola* and rowed to the safety of the stockade.

But the boat was overloaded and hard to steer. They saw in the distance that the big cannon was being set up on the ship's deck. Abraham Gray told them, to their dismay, that Israel Hands had been Flint's gunner.

Since the squire was the sharpest shooter in the group, he loaded his weapon and aimed at the ship. However, just as the squire fired, Israel Hands stooped down. The musket ball whistled over him, hitting one of the other four pirates.

Before the squire could load again, the great cannon roared and sent a cannonball toward the small boat. This must have been the first shot that Ben Gunn and I had heard. Luckily, the ball missed them, but the small boat rocked and tipped and sank in the shallow water. No one was hurt, but the supplies sank and only two guns were saved.

There was no time to lose, for they could hear

the voices of the pirates on the island coming nearer. The five men waded ashore as fast as they could. Just as the men had come up on the stockade, they saw the faces of seven pirates peering over the far corner of the high fence. Shots rang out on all sides. The pirates fired and Hunter and Joyce fired from inside the stockade. One of the enemy fell, and the rest turned and plunged into the trees.

The men began to rejoice at their success. But just then a pistol cracked, a ball whistled through the air, and poor Tom Redruth stumbled and fell on the ground. The squire and the doctor fired back, but did not know where to aim.

The captain and Gray bent over the squire's poor fallen gamekeeper. Carefully, they lifted him over the fence and carried him into the log blockhouse.

The squire dropped down beside him on his knees and kissed his hand, crying like a child. Redruth asked if he was dying, and the doctor told him that, yes, he was "going home." A prayer was said, and the faithful servant passed away.

In the meantime, the captain pulled two British flags from his coat. He had grabbed them, along with his logbook, a pen and some ink, before leaving the ship. He and Hunter propped up a fir tree log against a corner of the blockhouse. The captain climbed onto the roof and proudly attached the flag. Then he came into the blockhouse and draped the second flag over the body of Tom Redruth.

All through the evening, cannonballs roared and whistled through the air. Ball after ball flew over, or fell short, or kicked up the soft sand in the stockade. Only one ball popped in through the roof of the blockhouse and out again through the floor.

And it was at that moment that I had climbed the fence and come running toward the stockade, calling to my dear friends.

After I had heard the doctor's story, I told mine. The doctor was very interested in this man of the island, Ben Gunn.

"Is this Ben Gunn a good man?" he asked.

"I do not know, sir," said I. "And he may be crazy in the head."

"Ah," said the doctor, "a man who has been three years on a desert island, Jim, might not be in his right mind. That would be expected. Was it cheese you said he asked for?"

"Yes, sir, cheese," I answered.

"Well, Jim," says he, "I have a small piece of Parmesan cheese—a nice, hard cheese made in Italy. Well, that's for Ben Gunn!"

Life in the blockhouse was not pleasant. The cold evening breeze came in between the log walls. With the breeze came sand. There was sand in our eyes, sand in our teeth, and sand in our suppers. Our chimney was a square hole in the roof, and it did not let much smoke out. Most of the smoke stayed inside the blockhouse, making us cough and stinging our eyes.

But the good Captain Smollett kept us busy. He set up guard duties and had us take turns collecting firewood from outside the stockade. He kept our spirits up, though we knew our wise captain was unhappy.

"First ship I ever lost," he said.

We did not have much food inside the stockade. We knew it would be a month before a ship would be sent from Bristol to search for us. Our best hope, the captain said, was to kill off the pirates until they gave up or ran away with the *Hispaniola*. If they took the ship, we could search for more food and wait to be rescued.

The nineteen pirates were now down to about fourteen. We could hear them roaring and singing late into the night, camped down on the marshy shore. The doctor said many of the pirates would become sick with malaria before long.

I was dead tired, as you may imagine. When I got to sleep, I slept like a log of wood. Early the next morning, I awoke to the sound of voices.

"Flag of truce!" I heard someone say. Then with a cry of surprise, "It's Silver himself!"

And at that, up I jumped, rubbed my eyes, and ran to a loop-hole in the wall.

CHAPTER TWELVE

The Attack

Sure enough, there were two men outside the stockade. One of them was waving a white cloth. The other was Silver himself. They stood knee-deep in a low, white morning fog that had crawled out of the swamp.

"Ten to one this is a trick," said the captain. He called out, "Who goes? Stand, or we fire."

"Flag of truce," cried Silver.

"And what do you want with your flag of truce?" cried our captain.

"I'm Cap'n Silver, sir. I'm here to make a bargain," he shouted.

"*Cap'n Silver?* Who's he?" cried the captain.

Long John answered, "It's me, John Silver, sir. These lads have chosen me as their cap'n. All I ask is your word, Cap'n Smollett, to come to terms. Then let me go freely back."

"My man," said Captain Smollett, "I have not the slightest desire to talk to you. If you wish to talk to me, you can come, that's all."

"That's enough, cap'n," shouted Long John cheerily. "A word from you is enough."

Silver came to the fence, threw over his crutch, and got a leg up. With great strength and skill he climbed that fence and dropped to the other side.

Silver had terrible hard work getting up the steep land that led to the blockhouse. His crutch sank in the soft sand, but he stuck to it and at last arrived before the captain. Silver saluted. He was dressed up in a long blue coat with brass buttons. A fine hat was set on the back of his head.

"Here you are, my man," said Captain Smollett. "You had better sit down."

"You'll make me sit outside on the cold sand, cap'n?" complained Long John.

"Why, Silver, if you had been an *honest* sea cook, you might be treated better. But you're a common pirate—and here you'll sit."

"Well, well, cap'n," said the sea cook. He sat down on the sand. Then he spied me. "The top of the morning to you, Jim. The doctor, too! Why, there you all are together like a happy family."

"If you have anything to say, my man, better say it," said the captain.

"Right you are, Cap'n Smollett. Well now, that was a good trick last night. One of you is pretty handy with a handspike. But you won't be able to sneak over and kill another man again, I tell you."

The captain did not know what Silver was talking about—but I did! Ben Gunn must have paid a "late night visit" to the pirates while they lay about drunk. I reckoned that we now had one less enemy to deal with.

"Well, here it is," said Silver. "*We* want that treasure, and *you* want to save your lives. You have a map, haven't you?"

"Perhaps," replied the captain.

"Oh, well, you have, I know that," said Long John. "We want your map."

Here the two men smoked their pipes and eyed each other for quite a while.

"Now," Silver went on, "you give us the treasure map. You do that, and we'll offer you a choice.

Either you join us and we splits the treasure with you and drops you safely ashore somewheres. Or you can stay here, you can. We'll leave food and supplies with you. I'll give my word of honor to send a ship back here to pick you up."

Captain Smollett rose from his seat on the porch. "Is that all?" he said.

"Every last word, by thunder! If you refuse that, the next you'll see are musket balls."

"Very good," said the captain. "Now you'll hear me. If you'll come up one by one, unarmed, I'll take you home to a fair trial in England. If you won't, you have my word as an Englishman that I'll see you all to Davy Jones below. You can't find the treasure. You can't sail the ship. I stand here and tell you so. And they're the last good words you'll get from me. Now go, my lad, and double quick."

Silver's face turned red. "Give me a hand up!"

"Not I," said the captain.

"Who'll give me a hand up?" Silver roared.

Not a man moved. Growling, he crawled along the sand till he got hold of the porch and could get himself upon his crutch.

"Before an hour's out," he cried, "I'll crush your old blockhouse like a rum barrel."

And with a dreadful curse he stumbled off and plowed through the sand. The man with the flag of truce helped him over the fence—after four or five tries. Then he disappeared among the trees.

"To your posts," roared the captain. "Doctor, you take the door! Hunter, take the east side. Joyce, you stand by the west, my man. Mr. Trelawney, you are the best shot—you and Gray will take this long north side with the five loop-holes. Hawkins, neither you nor I are good at the shooting. We'll stand by to load muskets and give a hand."

The chill and the fog lifted. The sun began to bake the sand. We flung off our jackets and coats and rolled up our sleeves. Then we stood there in a fever of heat and fear. An hour passed away as we waited… and waited…

And then came the sounds of attack! Joyce whipped up his musket and fired. Shots rang out from all directions. Several bullets struck the blockhouse. Then all was quiet again until we heard a loud "Hurrah" as pirates leaped from the woods and ran straight to the stockade. A rifle ball sang through the doorway and knocked the doctor's musket into bits.

The pirates swarmed over the fence like monkeys. Squire and Gray fired again and again. Three pirates fell. Two had bit the dust, one had fled. But four had made it across the fence and into the stockade area. They ran for the blockhouse.

The rest of the pirates, still in the woods, shouted and cheered them on. In a moment, the four pirates were upon us.

The head of Job Anderson appeared at the middle loop-hole. "At 'em, all hands—all hands!" he roared in a voice of thunder.

At the same moment, another pirate grabbed Hunter's musket and pulled it through the loop-hole. With one blow, Hunter fell to the floor. Another pirate ran around to the doorway and fell with his cutlass on the doctor.

The blockhouse was full of gun smoke. I heard pistol shots and then one loud groan.

"Out, lads, out, and fight 'em in the open! Use your cutlasses!" cried the captain.

I grabbed a cutlass and dashed out of the door into the clear sunlight. Someone was close behind me! Right in front, the doctor was chasing an enemy down the hill.

The rest of the pirates were now swarming up the fence to make an end of us. One man was on the top with one leg over. He had on a red nightcap and held his cutlass in his mouth. But before he could climb over, the battle was finished—and victory was ours!

Gray had put an end to Job Anderson. Another pirate had been shot through a loop-hole while he tried to shoot into the blockhouse. The doctor struck a fatal blow to another. Of the four who had climbed the fence, only one was alive, and he was climbing back over the fence. In three seconds the attackers had fled. Five had been killed.

But we had paid a price for our victory. Hunter and Joyce both lay dead inside the blockhouse. The squire sat holding the captain, who had been hit by two musket balls.

"Have they run?" the captain asked weakly.

"All the ones that *could* run," answered the doctor. "But there's five of them that will never run again."

"Five!" cried the captain. "That leaves us our four men against their nine."

CHAPTER THIRTEEN

My Sea Adventure

The captain's shoulder blade and calf had been badly wounded. He would recover, the doctor said, but for weeks he must not walk nor move his arm.

After our meal, the squire and the doctor sat by the captain's side for a talk. Then the doctor grabbed his hat and pistols, strapped on a cutlass, and put the map in his pocket. With a musket over his shoulder, he climbed the fence and set off through the trees. I knew that he also carried some cheese and was headed to see ol' Ben Gunn.

The sun was fiercely hot. I longed for the cool shadow of the woods, away from all this blood and death. I needed to escape this place!

I decided to go find the large white rock where Ben Gunn had hidden a boat. I would slip out when nobody was watching, which I knew was wrong. But I was only a boy, and I had made my mind up. I filled my pockets with biscuits and grabbed two pistols, a powder horn and bullets. When the coast was clear, I made a bolt for it over the fence and into the thickest of the trees!

I ran down to the cove and looked out through the trees. I could see the *Hispaniola*, still flying the Jolly Roger. I crept out to the sandy area and crawled as quickly as I could toward the white rock. I reached it before the sun went down. Right below the rock I found a low place covered with high brush. Here I saw a little tent of goatskins. I lifted the side of the tent, and there was Ben Gunn's boat—a homemade, lop-sided round boat made of wood and goatskin. It was very small, even for me.

Until then, I had never seen a coracle—this type of round boat made by primitive people. But I can say that Ben Gunn's boat was the worst coracle ever made by man.

Yet this strange little boat gave me my next wild idea. I would slip out at night, cut the *Hispaniola* loose from her anchor, and let her drift ashore!

Down I sat to wait for darkness and eat some biscuits. When night came, I waded into the water with my coracle and set myself to sea.

The coracle was impossible to steer. No matter how I tried, I could not get her to go straight. Turning round and round was what she did best. Even when I paddled, she turned in every direction but the one I aimed for. Luckily, the tide pulled me toward the *Hispaniola.* I came alongside of her anchor rope and laid hold. I sliced at the rope with my knife until I had cut the last fibers.

Curiosity then grabbed hold of me and I grabbed hold of the rope. I pulled myself up hand over hand until I could see into the cabin. There was Israel Hands wrestling with the man in the red nightcap. Each had a hand upon the other's throat! I dropped back down, frightened by the scene.

I could see the glow of the pirates' campfire on shore and hear them singing the song I knew well:

Fifteen men on the dead man's chest—
Yo-ho-ho, and a bottle of rum!

Suddenly, my little coracle tipped in the water and pushed me toward the hull of the *Hispaniola*! I lay down flat in the bottom of that awful little boat, prayed, and got ready to meet my maker.

I must have lain like that for hours, waiting for death. I could feel the coracle being beaten by waves and I was drenched with sea spray. Sleep fell upon me and I dreamed of home.

I woke to find that I had drifted out of the cove. My throat was dry. All round me was salty water that I could not drink. The sun beat down on me and my brain ached. The spray of seawater caked my lips with salt. I bailed water out with my sea cap, and dreaded drifting out to the open sea.

Then I saw, not half a mile away, the *Hispaniola*. I knew I would be spotted—but I was so thirsty that I was glad of this. I wondered how the ship could have drifted so far. The men on board must be dead or drunk, I thought. Or maybe they had deserted the ship. Perhaps if I could get on board I could steer the ship and return her to her captain.

I drifted closer to the ship. What if there *were* still men on board? And how tall she looked to me from down in my coracle! But I laid aside my fears and waited for my chance. A large swell lifted my boat. I sprang to my feet and leaped, which pushed my coracle under water. I caught the jib-boom and clung there, panting. I had now lost the coracle and was left with no way off the *Hispaniola*.

I tumbled headfirst upon the deck. All along the side of the deck I saw empty bottles. And then, sure enough, I saw two drunk—or maybe dead—pirates. "Redcap" was as stiff as a handspike. Israel Hands was propped against the side, his chin on his chest, his face as white as a wax candle.

The ship was being jostled about by the waves and the wind that caught her sails. At every jump of the ship, the men swayed back and forth but gave no sign of life. I saw splashes of blood on the deck and was sure that they had killed each other.

But then, while I was looking and wondering, Israel Hands turned partly around! With a low moan he sat up. I knew he must be in great pain, and at first I felt sorry for him. But when I remembered the talk I had overheard from the apple barrel, all pity left me.

"Come aboard, Mr. Hands," I said with a slow, sly smile.

CHAPTER FOURTEEN

Israel Hands

Hands rolled his eyes around and stared at me. "Much hurt?" I asked him.

He grunted, "I don't have no luck, and that's what's the matter with me." He nodded toward the man with the red cap. "As for *that* swab, he's good and dead, he is. O'Brien warn't no sailor, anyhow. And where might *you* have come from?"

"Well," said I, "I've come aboard to take this ship, Mr. Hands. You'll please call me Captain."

He looked at me sourly but said nothing.

"By the bye," I said, pointing to the Jolly Roger, "I can't have these colors, Mr. Hands. I'll strike 'em. Better none than these."

I ran to the flag lines, brought down their black flag, and chucked it overboard.

"God save the King!" said I, waving my cap.

He watched me keenly and slyly. "I reckon, Cap'n Hawkins," he said, "you'll want to get ashore now. S'pose we talks."

"Why, with all my heart, Mr. Hands. Say on."

"Now, look here, you gives me food and drink and a old 'ankerchief to tie my wound up, and I'll tell you how to sail her."

"I'm not going back to the cove," says I. "We'll sail into North Inlet and beach her quietly there."

"North Inlet? Why, I'll help you sail her there, I will," he said.

We struck our bargain on the spot. In three minutes I had the *Hispaniola* sailing easily along the western coast toward the North Inlet that I had seen on the map. Then I went below to my own cabin where I got a soft silk handkerchief of my mother's. I bound up Hands' great bleeding stab wound in his thigh. I drank some cool water and ate some biscuits. Both of us were feeling better.

The breeze served us well. Soon we had turned the corner of the rocky hill that ends the island on the north.

I was enjoying my role as captain. I had plenty of water and good things to eat. The weather was pleasant. The only thing that bothered me was Israel Hands' odd smile as he watched, and watched, and watched me at my work.

We reached the North Inlet, but, of course, had no anchor to let down. In order to beach the ship, we would have to wait for the tide to go out.

We both sat in silence over a meal. Then Hands said with his same strange smile, "This here's an unlucky ship, this *Hispaniola*, Jim. I never seen such dirty luck, not I. There was this here O'Brien, now—he's dead, ain't he? Do you take it as a dead man is dead for good, or do he come alive again?"

"You can kill the body, Mr. Hands, but not the spirit," I replied. "O'Brien there is in another world, and may be watching us."

"Ah!" says he. "Well, I do know one thing, I do. Dead men don't bite. That's my view—amen, so be it. Now, Jim, I'll take it kind if you'd step down into that there cabin and get me a bottle of wine."

I knew he just wanted me to leave the deck. He wouldn't look me in the eye.

"All right, Mr. Hands," I answered, "but I'll have to dig for it."

I scuttled down the stairs and tried to make a lot of noise. Then I slipped off my shoes, ran quietly along the next ladder, and popped my head out of the opening beyond him.

He was on his hands and knees! I watched as he pulled himself across the deck and picked a bloody dirk—a ten-inch knife—out of a coil of rope. He hid it in his jacket and crawled back to his old place.

So! Israel Hands could move about, and he was now armed with a dirk.

I quietly crept back, slipped into my shoes, and grabbed a bottle of wine. I came up the ladder and found Hands just as I had left him.

"Here's luck!" he said, taking a swig of the wine. "The tide's out now. You just take my orders, Cap'n Hawkins, and we'll sail slap in and be done with it."

I was a good sub-captain, and Hands was an excellent pilot. "Starboard a little—so—steady," he commanded, "—starboard—larboard a little. Steady—steady!" We went about and about and dodged in near the shore. "Now, my hearty, luff!"

I pulled hard and the *Hispaniola* swung round rapidly and went straight for the sandy shore. With all the excitement I forgot to watch Hands. When I looked round, he was already halfway toward me with the dirk in his right hand!

We both cried out when our eyes met. Mine was the shrill cry of terror. His was a roar of fury like a charging bull's. He lunged forward and I leaped sideways. I drew a pistol from my belt, took a cool aim, and drew the trigger—but there was no flash! The powder was wet from the seawater! Why had I not cleaned and reloaded my only weapons?

Although he was wounded, Hands moved quickly. His grizzled hair tumbled over his red, furious face. I knew my pistols were useless, and I knew I could be boxed in against the side of the ship. If that happened, nine or ten inches of the bloodstained dirk would be my last experience on this side of life. I placed my palms against the main mast and waited—every nerve upon the stretch.

Hands also paused. He moved to the right. I moved to the left. Right. Left. Back again. It was like two boys at play dodging around the rocks back home at Black Hill Cove. But, you may be sure, no boy's heart had ever beat so wildly. I saw no hope of any escape.

Suddenly, the *Hispaniola* struck the beach. The ship shook and leaned over on her side. Water splashed onto the deck. We were tossed in an instant and rolled, almost together, down the deck. The dead Redcap tumbled stiffly after us. My head hit Israel Hands' foot with a crack that made my teeth rattle. I got to my feet, but Hands was tangled with the dead body. I could not run on the tilted deck—and Hands was coming at me with his dirk!

Quick as thought, I sprang into the mizzen shrouds, climbed up hand over hand, and did not draw a breath till I was seated on the cross-trees. The dirk had struck the mast not half a foot below me—and there stood Israel Hands with his mouth open and his face looking up at mine.

Now that I had a moment to myself, I loaded my pistols. But Hands had also hauled himself into the shrouds. With the dirk in his teeth, he began slowly and painfully to climb.

With a pistol in either hand, I addressed him.

"One more step, Mr. Hands," said I, "and I'll shoot! Dead men don't bite, you know."

He stopped instantly. I could see by his face that he was trying to think, and this was a slow process for him. His expression made me laugh aloud.

He took the dirk from his mouth and said, "Jim, I don't have no luck, not I. But I reckon I'll have to strike. That comes hard, you see, for a master sailor to kill a good boy like you, Jim."

I was smiling, listening to him and feeling cocky, when, in a flash, back went his right hand over his shoulder. Something sang like an arrow through the air. I felt a blow and then a sharp pang! And there I was, pinned by the shoulder to the mast.

In the horrid pain and surprise of the moment, both my pistols went off, and both dropped out of my hands. They did not fall alone. With a choked cry, Israel Hands let go of the shrouds and plunged headfirst into the water.

From my perch on the leaning cross-trees, I could see him lying on the clean, bright sand, as fishes swam over and around him.

I felt sick, faint, and terrified. Hot blood was running over my back and chest. The dirk that

pinned my shoulder to the mast burned like a hot iron. I clung with both hands till my nails ached, and I shut my eyes until I could regain my senses.

The thought of pulling the dirk from my shoulder made me shudder. Oddly enough, the knife only held me by a mere pinch of skin, and the shudder tore the skin loose. I ripped my shirt away from the knife and climbed down the shrouds to the deck.

I went below to my cabin and tended to my wound. Then I cleared the deck of its last passenger—the dead man, O'Brien. With one good heave, I tumbled him overboard. I could see him and Israel lying side by side under the water and the quick fishes steering to and fro over them.

CHAPTER FIFTEEN

"Pieces of Eight"

I was now alone upon the ship. The sun was setting and the sails were flapping in the evening breeze. I pulled down as many sails as I could so that they would not tear in the wind. I had to leave half of them attached.

I scurried down the cut anchor rope, softly dropped into the waist-deep water, and waded ashore. I looked back at the *Hispaniola*. There she lay on her side with her main sail trailing in the bay. But she was clear at last from pirates and ready for our own men to board and get to sea again. I couldn't wait to get to the stockade and boast of my tales.

Gradually the night fell blacker. The stars were few and pale. The bright moon rose over Spyglass Hill and lit my way. I came to the fence and looked into the stockade. Not a soul stirred. All was quiet.

I climbed over the fence and crawled toward the blockhouse. Then I heard a wonderful sound—the snoring of my friends. At the doorway I stood up and slowly walked through the darkness. With a silent chuckle, I pictured my friends' faces when they would wake in the morning and find me there.

My foot struck something—it was a sleeper's leg. He turned and groaned. And then, all of a sudden, a shriek broke forth out of the darkness:

"Pieces of eight! Pieces of eight! Pieces of eight! Pieces of eight! Pieces of eight!"

Silver's green parrot, Captain Flint! I had no time to think. The sleepers awoke and sprang up. The voice of Silver cried, "Who goes?"

I turned, ran against one person, turned again, and ran full into the arms of someone else.

"Bring a torch, Dick," said Silver.

One of the men left and returned with a lighted torch. The red glare lit up the blockhouse. There I saw six ill-looking pirates—and none of my friends!

There sat the parrot on Long John's shoulder.

"So," said he, "here's Jim Hawkins, shiver my timbers! Dropped in, like, eh? Quite a pleasant surprise for poor old John."

I made no answer. My back was against the wall. I looked Silver in the face, trying to look brave.

Silver sat down and filled his pipe. "I've always liked you, Jim, I have," he said. "You're the picture of my own self when I was young and handsome. I always wanted you to join us. Your friends think you've left them. 'Ungrateful scamp' was what the doctor said. They won't have you, now. You'll have to join with Cap'n Silver."

"You need an answer, then?" I asked with a trembling voice. My heart beat painfully in my chest. "Well, I have a right to know why you're here, and where my friends are."

One of the pirates growled and came at me, but Silver held him back and calmly said, "Yesterday morning, Mr. Hawkins, Doctor Livesey came to our camp with a flag of truce. Says he, 'Cap'n Silver, the ship's gone.' We looked out, and by thunder, the old ship was gone! 'Well,' says the doctor, 'let's bargain.' We bargained, him and I, and here we are. We have the blockhouse. As for your mates, they've gone off. I don't know where they are."

He quietly smoked his pipe.

"And now I am to choose?" said I.

"And now you are to choose," said Silver.

"Well," said I, "there's a thing or two I have to tell you. Here you are—ship lost, treasure lost, men lost. And if you want to know who did it—it was I! I was in the apple barrel the night we sighted land, and I heard you, John, and you, Dick Johnson, and Hands, who is now at the bottom of the sea, and told every word you said. And as for the ship, it was I who cut her loose and it was I who brought her where you'll never see her more, not one of you. The laugh's on my side. I no more fear you than I fear a fly. Kill me, if you please, or spare me. But one thing I'll say—if you spare me, then we'll forget the past. And when you fellows are in court for being pirates, I'll save you all if I can. It is for you to choose."

I was out of breath. The men sat staring at me like sheep. Then one sprang at me with a knife.

"Avast, Tom Morgan!" cried Silver. "Maybe you thought you was cap'n here. Cross me, and you'll go to Davy Jones below to feed the fishes."

Morgan paused. The pirates murmured angrily.

"I like that boy, now," Silver went on. "He's more a man than any pair of rats of you in this here house. You'll not lay a hand on him."

My heart was still going like a sledge hammer.

Silver kept an eye on all the men, who went to the back of the room and talked in whispers.

"Pipe up and let me hear you," snapped Silver.

A yellow-eyed man spoke up. "Sir, this crew's dissatisfied. This crew has rights like other crews. And this crew wants to step outside for a council."

One by one, the pirates saluted Silver and left the blockhouse. I was alone with Silver.

"Now, look you here, Jim Hawkins," he said in a steady whisper, "I know the game is up, and that I'll have to join back with the squire. As for that council, why, they'll depose me of bein' captain, they will. They're fools and cowards. But I'll save your life from them, lad, if you save Long John from hanging after I join back with your men."

"What I can do, that I'll do," I said.

"It's a bargain!" cried Long John. "Understand me, Jim. I know you've got that ship safe somewheres. How you done it, I don't know, but safe it is. And you and me—we might have done a power of good together!" He paused. "Tell me, Jim, why did that doctor give me the map?"

My face and mind went blank with surprise.

"Ah, well, he did, though," said Silver. "And there's something fishy to that, Jim, there is."

The door opened, and the five men came in. One man was pushed forward.

"Step up, lad," cried Silver. "I won't eat you. Hand it over. I know the rules, I do."

The young man passed something to Silver.

"The black spot! I thought so," Silver said.

"See what's wrote there," said George Merry, the man with the yellow eyes. "Then you can talk."

"Thanky, George. Well, what is it, anyway? Ah! 'Deposed'—that's it, is it? Did you write it, George? You'll be voted cap'n next, I'm sure."

"You're over now, Silver, and you'll maybe step down off that barrel and help vote."

"I'm still the captain till I've had my chance to talk," roared Silver. "After that, we'll see."

"You've made a hash of this cruise," snarled George Merry. "You let the enemy go—for nothing! Then, you wouldn't let us go at them as they left. And there's this here boy…"

"Is that all?" asked Silver quietly. Then he raised his voice. "Look here, I'll answer to you. Who was it that elected me captain? All of you here. And if you had done like I said at first, we'd have that treasure and the ship, too. I'm sick to speak to you. I don't know why yer mothers let you come to sea!"

Silver was shouting by now. He wiped sweat from his brow.

"So ya don't like my bargain with the enemy, eh? You don't even *know* my bargain! The doctor has agreed to come tend to this ragged lot. You, George—you're feverish from malaria. Your eyes are the color of lemon peel. You, there, with your head broke—you'll be glad when the doctor comes. And this boy here? Why, shiver my timbers, isn't he a hostage? Kill that boy? Not me, mates! When the rescue ship comes, we'll be glad to have this here hostage! And now as to why I made the bargain with the squire… well, you came crawling on your knees to me to make it, you was so starved and sick. And there's more—I got *this* in the bargain!"

And he threw something down on the floor—it was the map! The pirates leaped upon that map like cats. They laughed and hooted and shouted, "Hooray for Silver! Barbecue for Cap'n!"

"George, I reckon you'll have to wait another turn, friend," said Silver.

That was the end of that awful night. Silver stayed as captain, and I stayed alive.

CHAPTER SIXTEEN

The Doctor's Visit

We were awakened the next morning by a clear, hearty voice calling, "Ahoy! Here's the doctor."

I ran to a loop-hole. Sure enough, it was the doctor. I felt ashamed to have him see me.

"Top o' the morning to you, sir!" cried Silver. "George, help Doctor Livesey over. Your patients are happy to see ya, Doctor. And we've quite a surprise for you, too, sir. We've a little stranger here—hee! hee! Slept right alongside of me, he did."

Dr. Livesey was over the fence and had come up to Silver. "Not Jim?" I heard him say.

"The very same Jim as ever was," said Silver.

They came in. The doctor gave me a grim nod, but went straight to work with the sick men. He gave out medicine and changed bandages, as if he were making a family visit. The fever, he said, came from sleeping in this horrid swamp. He finished his rounds, then spoke to Silver.

"Well, that's done for today. And now I wish to have a talk with that boy, please."

There was an uproar from the men, but Silver silenced them. He spoke quietly with the doctor, then said to me, "Hawkins, will you give me your word of honor not to slip your cable?"

I gave him my pledge not to run.

Silver told the doctor to go on over the fence. He barked to the grumbling men to get ready for the treasure hunt. Then, slowly, slowly, Silver and I made our way down to the fence. Once out of earshot, Silver explained to the doctor that he was once again on their side. He told how he saved my life, and asked if the doctor and the squire would speak well of him if he went to trial for piracy.

"You'll forget the bad, now won't you, Doctor?" Silver asked with sad, pleading eyes. Then he stepped back, sat upon a stump and whistled as he watched us and the blockhouse.

"So, Jim," said the doctor sadly, "here you are. How could you run off? With Captain Smollett ill?"

I will admit that I began to weep. "Doctor," I said, "you might spare me. I'm good as dead anyway. If they torture me—"

"Jim," the doctor interrupted, "Jim, I can't have this. Whip over, and we'll run for it."

"Doctor," said I, "I gave my word. You know right well you wouldn't break *your* word—neither you nor squire nor captain. Nor will I. But, Doctor, you did not let me finish. If they torture me, I might let slip a word of where the ship is, for I got the ship, and she lies in North Inlet."

"The ship!" exclaimed the doctor.

Quickly I described to him my adventures. After some silence, he said, "At every step, it's you that saves our lives, Jim, and do you suppose that we are going to let you lose yours? You overheard the plot. You found Ben Gunn—Oh, and speaking of Ben Gunn…" Seeing Silver walk over, he called out, "Silver! Silver! I'll give you a piece of advice. Don't you be in any great hurry after that treasure."

"Why, sir," said Silver, "I can only save my life and the boy's by seeking for that treasure."

"Well, I'll not tell more," said the doctor. "But I *will* say, Silver, if we both get off this island, I'll do my best to save you from being hung for piracy."

Silver's face was radiant. "You couldn't say more, sir, if you was my own mother," he cried.

"Hear well my advice, Silver. Keep the boy close. And when you need help, call out 'Halloo.' I'm off to find help now. Good-bye, Jim."

Dr. Livesey shook hands with me through the fence, nodded to Silver, and set off at a brisk pace into the woods.

"Jim," said Silver when we were alone, "I saved your life. You saved mine. I'll not forget it. I seen the doctor waving you to run for it—and I seen you say no. And now, Jim, we're to go in for this here treasure hunting, and I don't like it. You and me must stick close to save our necks."

CHAPTER SEVENTEEN

The Treasure Hunt

At breakfast, Silver announced, "Aye, mates, I learned that they've hid the ship. But once we hit the treasure, we'll jump into our jolly-boats and take that ship, we will. Until then, Mister Hawkins here will be our hostage. I'll take him in a line when we go treasure hunting."

The men were cheered, but I was downcast. I knew Silver would never join the squire if the pirates *did* get the treasure and the ship.

I still could not understand why my friends had left the stockade. Why had they given the pirates the map? And what did the doctor's warning mean—that Silver should not be in a hurry to find the treasure? With an uneasy heart, I left with the pirates on the treasure hunt.

We were an odd-looking bunch. The men carried picks and shovels and food and wore ragged clothes. All were armed to the teeth, except me. Silver had two guns slung about him, besides the great cutlass at his waist and a pistol in each pocket of his square-tailed coat. Captain Flint sat perched upon his shoulder, gabbling sea talk. I had a rope about my waist and followed after Silver, who held the loose end of the rope—sometimes in his hand, sometimes in his teeth. For all the world, I was led like a dancing bear.

We straggled to the beach where the two jolly-boats awaited us. The plan was to row them to a landing spot close to where the treasure was marked on the map and then follow the map clues:

Tall tree, Spyglass shoulder,
bearing a point to the N. of N.N.E.
Skeleton Island E.S.E. and by E.   *Ten feet.*

We landed at the mouth of the river that runs down the side of Spyglass Hill. There we got out and began our climb through the swampy ground.

The land became steeper and stonier. Then we came to an area of sweet-smelling shrubs and thickets of nutmeg trees. Right before us was a flat area with tall pine trees, on the shoulder of Spyglass Hill. One of these trees had to be the "tall tree" of Flint's map.

The men spread out, shouting and leaping to and fro. I followed behind Long John Silver. From time to time I had to help him, or he would have missed his footing and fallen down the hill.

After half a mile, we came to the edge of the flat area. Suddenly, one of the men began to cry out as if in terror. We ran forward, thinking the treasure was found—but then a chill struck every heart.

There at the foot of a big pine lay a human skeleton, grown over with vines. The skeleton lay perfectly straight. His feet pointed in one direction. His hands were raised above his head like a diver's, pointing in the other direction.

Silver was the only one calm. "I'm thinking..." he said. "The tip top point o' Skeleton Island seems to lie right along the line of them bones."

The men checked the compass, and sure enough, the body pointed straight in the direction of the island, and the compass read E.S.E. and by E.

"I thought so," cried Silver. "This here is a pointer—one of *Flint's* jokes. It makes me cold to think of it. Him and those six was alone here, and he killed 'em all. This one he hauled here and laid down as a pointer, shiver my timbers!"

"I saw Flint die with my own eyes," said Morgan.

"Dead—aye, sure enough he's dead and gone below," said another. "But if ever a spirit walked, it would be Flint's. He died bad, did Flint!"

"Aye, that he did," said another. "First he raged, then he called for rum, then he sang, 'Fifteen men on the dead man's chest.' He turned blue, he did."

"Come, come," said Silver, "stow this talk. He's dead, and his spirit don't walk. Ahead to the gold!"

We started, but the pirates kept side by side and spoke in frightened whispers.

Before us stood Spyglass Hill with many tall pine trees and cliffs. Silver took out his compass. "There are three 'tall trees' to check, " said he. "It should be easy enough to find the stuff now."

"I don't feel easy," growled Morgan. "Thinkin' o' Flint, I think, has done me."

"He were an ugly devil," cried another pirate.

All of a sudden, out of the trees in front of us a high, trembling voice sang out:

Fifteen men on the dead man's chest—
Yo-ho-ho, and a bottle of rum!

I never have seen men more scared than those pirates. The color went from their six faces. Some leaped to their feet, some clawed hold of others. Morgan groveled on the ground.

"It's Flint!" cried George Merry.

The song stopped as suddenly as it began.

"Come," said Silver, in a shaky voice. "This won't do. I can't name the voice, but it's someone playing, you can bet on that."

But then the same voice began wailing, "Darby M'Graw! Darby M'Graw!' again and again and again. Then a little higher, "Fetch the rum, Darby!"

The pirates were in absolute terror.

"They was Flint's last words," moaned Morgan.

"That fixes it!" gasped one. "Let's go."

"Shipmates," Silver cried, "I'm here to get that gold, and I'll not be beat by man or devil. I never feared Flint in his life, and I'll face him dead. There's a treasure in gold not a quarter of a mile from here! I tell ya, that weren't Flint's spirit!"

"Come to think on it," said Merry, "it wasn't just like Flint's voice, after all. It was more like somebody else's voice—more like—"

"By thunder, Ben Gunn!" roared Silver.

"Aye, and so it were," cried Morgan. "Ben Gunn's spirit it were!"

"Why, nobody minds Ben Gunn," cried Merry. "Dead or alive, nobody minds him."

Soon they were chatting together and setting forth again. It was fine open walking up here. We could see out over the water (where I had tossed and trembled in the coracle).

After checking a couple tall pines, we saw one that rose nearly two hundred feet into the air. This had to be *the* tall tree! Somewhere beneath its shadow lay seven hundred thousand in gold! The thought of the money erased any terror the men had felt. Their eyes burned in their heads. Their feet grew speedier just thinking of the treasure that lay waiting for each of them.

Silver hobbled, grunting, on his crutch. He cursed like a madman when the flies settled on his hot face. From time to time he yanked the rope and gave me a deadly look. I knew his thoughts. If he found gold, he would forget his promise to me and the doctor. He planned to seize the treasure, find the *Hispaniola*, cut every honest throat on that island, and sail away.

We were now at the edge of a thicket.

"Hurrah, mates, all together!" shouted Merry.

They broke into a run—but then we saw them all stop. A low cry arose. Silver doubled his pace, digging away with the foot of his crutch. In the next moment he and I also came to a dead halt.

Before us was a deep pit. Down inside was a broken pick-axe and boards from broken crates. All was clear. The treasure had already been found. The seven hundred thousand in gold was gone!

The men looked like they had been struck. But I could see Silver's face—hatching a new plan.

"Jim," he whispered, "take that, and stand by."

He passed me a double-barreled pistol. Slowly he led me to the other side of the pit. I could not help whispering, "So you've changed sides again."

The pirates cried and leaped into the pit to dig with their fingers. Morgan found one small coin.

"One coin!" he roared, shaking it at Silver. "That's your seven hundred thousand, is it?"

"Dig away, boys," said Silver with a cool voice. "You'll find some coppers, I should guess."

"Coppers!" screamed Merry. "Mates, do you hear that? I tell you now, that man there knew it all along. Look at his face!"

"Ah, George," said Silver, "are you standing in as captain again?"

By this time, the others had scrambled out of the pit and stood with Merry.

Well, there we stood, two on one side, five on the other, the pit between us. Silver never moved. He watched them, upright on his crutch, and looked as cool as ever I saw him.

"Mates," says Merry, "there's two of them alone there. One's the old cripple that's blundered this whole thing. The other's that cub that I mean to have the heart of. Now, mates—"

He was raising his arm and his voice, when— crack! crack! crack!—three musket shots flashed out of the thicket. Merry tumbled headfirst into the pit. The man with the bandage spun round like a top and fell on his side. The other three turned and ran for it with all their might.

Before you could wink, Long John sent a shot into the struggling Merry. "George," said Silver, "I reckon I settled you."

At the same moment, the doctor, Gray, and Ben Gunn joined us, with smoking muskets, from out of the thicket.

CHAPTER EIGHTEEN

And Last

"Forward!" cried the doctor. "After 'em—they're headed to the boats!"

We set off, plunging through the bushes.

I tell you, Silver was anxious to keep up with us. He leaped on his crutch till the muscles of his chest were fit to burst. From behind us he called out, "Doctor, see there! No hurry!"

We could see the three men running right for Mizzenmast Hill. We were already between them and the boats, and so we sat down to breathe.

"Thanky kindly, Doctor," Silver said, mopping his face. "You came in the nick of time for me and Hawkins." Then he added, "So it's you, Ben Gunn!"

"I'm Ben Gunn, I am," replied the maroon, wriggling like an eel. "And, how do, Mr. Silver? Pretty well, I thank ye, says you."

"Ben, Ben," murmured Silver, "to think as you've done me!"

As we walked down to the boats, the doctor told us Ben Gunn's story, and what happened after he himself had gone to find Gunn that morning. Ben Gunn was the hero from beginning to end.

In his long, lonely wanderings about the island, Gunn had found the skeleton—and the treasure. He had dug it up and carried it on his back, in many weary journeys, from the foot of the tall pine to a cave he had at the northeast of the island. There it was safely stored—and this he had told the doctor.

When the doctor saw that the ship was no longer in the cove (thanks to me!) he had gone to Silver to make a bargain. He asked that the pirates allow the squire's crew to leave the stockade in peace. In return, the doctor gave Silver the map (which was now useless) and promised food and supplies and medicine for the sick men. The bargain was made. My friends had left the stockade and headed to Ben Gunn's cave.

The doctor had gotten Gray and Gunn to go with him to the site of the tall pine and the pit. Gunn ran ahead to stall his old shipmates, singing and calling out the words of Flint.

When we came to the jolly-boats, we destroyed one, and got aboard the other to row the eight miles to North Inlet. We passed the mouth of Ben Gunn's cave, and saw the squire waving to us. We all gave him three cheers—including Silver.

Three miles farther, what should we meet but the *Hispaniola*, afloat and drifting! As it was, she was in good shape except for the main sail. We attached another anchor and dropped it over. Then we rowed round near the cave and hiked up.

The squire met us, glaring at Silver. "John Silver, I am told I am not to let you hang. But you're a monstrous villain and imposter."

"Thanky kindly, sir," replied Silver, saluting.

The cave was a large, airy place overhung with ferns. Captain Smollett lay before a nice fire. In a far corner lay great heaps of coins and stacks of gold bars. Flint's treasure! Later, I would help to pack the coins. It was a strange collection, much like the coins that Billy Bones had. English, French, Spanish, doubloons and "pieces of eight." There were round pieces, square pieces, and pieces with holes in the middle—nearly every kind of money in the world, I think. Sadly, I thought of the seventeen from our crew that had died for that treasure.

What a meal I had with my friends that night, with salted goat and a bottle of old wine from the *Hispaniola*. Never were people brighter or happier. And there was Silver—joining in the laughter, and lending a hand, just like in his sea cook days.

The next morning we began to cart the gold to the jolly-boat. Gray and Gunn then made trips to the ship. Day after day this work went on—with no sign of the three pirates. On the third night, the doctor and I heard their far-off singing. "Drunk," said Silver. "Malaria," said the doctor. A council was held, and it was decided that we must desert them on the island—to the huge glee, I must say, of Ben Gunn. We left a good stock of gunpowder and shot, most of the salted goat, a few medicines, some tools, clothing, a spare sail, and rope.

At last, one fine morning, we pulled up the anchor. High above flew the flag that the captain had flown and fought under at the stockade.

Rounding the island, we saw something that grabbed our hearts. All three of the marooned men were kneeling with their arms raised, calling, "For God's sake, don't leave us to die in such a place." The doctor shouted out where we had left food and supplies. One leaped to his feet with a hoarse cry and sent a musket shot whistling over Silver's head and through the main sail.

That was, at least, the end of that. Before noon, to my joy, the highest rock of Treasure Island had sunk into the blue round of sea.

We all worked double shifts and safely sailed to Spanish America. The doctor, the squire and I went ashore to the happy faces of the islanders and the wonderful sights and smells of tropical fruits.

When we returned to the *Hispaniola*, Ben Gunn told us that Silver was gone. He had gotten one of the sacks of coins and slipped away. I think we were all pleased to be so cheaply rid of him.

Well, to make a long story short, we got a few new hands on board and reached Bristol just as Mr. Blandly was thinking of sending a rescue ship.

All of us had a share of the treasure. Captain Smollett is now retired from the sea. Gray not only saved his money, but he is now part owner of a fine full-rigged ship, married besides, and the father of a family. As for Ben Gunn, he spent or lost his share in three weeks, so the squire gave him a gatekeeper's job. Folks make fun of his ways, but he has become a favorite singer in church on Sundays.

Of Silver we have heard no more. That seafaring man with one leg has at last gone clean out of my life. I would guess he lives in comfort with a wife and his parrot, Captain Flint.

For all I know, the rest of the silver bars and the

weapons marked on the map still lie where Flint buried them. Certainly I will never look for them. Oxen and ropes would not bring me back to that accursed island. And the worst dreams I ever have are when I hear the surf booming about its coasts or spring upright in bed with the sharp voice of Captain Flint still ringing in my ears: "Pieces of eight! Pieces of eight!"

Pieces of eight!

Pieces of eight!

Pieces of eight!

Pieces of eight!

Pieces of eight!

ROBERT LOUIS STEVENSON

Robert Louis Stevenson was born in Edinburgh, Scotland, in 1850, into a family of lighthouse engineers. Robert loved the sea. While studying law at the University of Edinburgh, he discovered another love—writing.

Stevenson had been sickly and frail since childhood, and his family worried about his health. Despite these concerns, Stevenson went on to achieve great success as a writer.

Stevenson traveled, in search of adventure and a climate that might ease his poor health. He married an American, Fanny Osbourne, who shared his love of travel and supported his writing. Stevenson sketched a map of a treasure island for his stepson Lloyd, one day, who asked that he write a story about it—and *Treasure Island* was published in 1883. He also wrote *The Strange Case of Dr. Jekyll and Mr. Hyde* (1886), and *Kidnapped* (1886).

Stevenson moved to the South Pacific island of Samoa to improve his health. However, in 1894 at the age of 44, he died there and was buried on a hillside overlooking the sea he loved.